LIFFEY RIVERS

FOUR MINI MYSTERIES

BRENNA BRIGGS

2012

ISBN: 1461103010
ISBN-13: 978-1461103011

DEDICATION

For Patsy, Loyola and Anthony

CONTENTS

Author Brenna Briggs has created the perfect series of adventures for Irish dancers.

London: The Irish World

These short stories were previously published in *Irish Dancing and Culture Magazine*. Many thanks to editors Tamasine, Lucy and Tallulah. Also to Nicola for her help and encouragement.

.

THE WEREWOLVES OF OSSORY

Liffey Rivers snapped her phone shut impatiently. Aunt Jean had missed the plane from Milwaukee to Seattle. "Why am I not surprised?" Liffey grumbled.

After an exhausting trip, which had begun at 5:00 a.m., Liffey had finally arrived in Seattle, Washington, from Pittsburgh, Pennsylvania, by way of Houston, Texas. She had hoped to meet up with her Aunt Jean and go straight to the feis hotel to practice her Irish dance steps for the Halloween Feis the next day.

Aunt Jean was supposed to meet her at the airport and they would travel together to their downtown Seattle hotel. Liffey's father, Attorney Robert Rivers, did not want her traveling alone to a feis so far away from home. After much discussion ("Seattle is simply too far away for an eleven-year-old girl like you to stay all by yourself in a hotel without supervision."), Liffey had agreed with her father's demand that her weird aunt would accompany her every step of the way.

Aunt Jean had previously accompanied Liffey to only one other competition—in Illinois. Liffey still cringed when she remembered how her aunt had embarrassed her there. Aunt Jean had worn black stiletto heels that tore up the manicured lawns as she spiked around the feis grounds and it looked like she had used a permanent black magic marker for her eyeliner. A pathetic, black sun hat and too-tight jeans completed her aunt's hideous wardrobe ensemble.

Aunt Jean was a former cheerleader and did not seem to understand that Irish dance was not a pom pom squad. After Liffey had explained to her aunt that yelling: "Kick 'em High, Kick 'em Low, Liffey! Liffey! GO! GO! GO!" while she was dancing was totally inappropriate and banned at feiseanna, Aunt Jean had promised she would never cheer for Liffey again.

After that disaster, Liffey made her father promise not to *ever* again let her aunt accompany her to another feis. It was not that she did not love and respect her aunt. She did. She just never wanted her aunt anywhere near a feis stage again. Liffey had enough to worry about at a feis without worrying about what her peculiar Aunt Jean was going to do or say next.

And now here she was, waiting for Aunt Jean to turn up in Seattle for the Halloween Feis.

Liffey very much wished now that she had accepted the generous offer from the nice woman sitting next to her on the plane when she had offered to drive her to the feis hotel. However, since this friendly woman was technically a stranger, even though Liffey felt like she had known her forever, Liffey had declined the offer.

The woman wore a beautiful diamond 'M' necklace and she knew how to Irish dance and had given Liffey great tips on how to improve her foot extension in the Houston airport after they ate big bowls of chili together. The diamond 'M' lady had even offered to take Liffey to tour the Seattle Space Needle while she waited for her aunt. Reluctantly, Liffey had turned down the offer because she had been trained long ago never to go off with anyone if she had not been properly introduced. Never.

Waiting in the Seattle-Tacoma Airport terminal for her unreliable Aunt Jean to turn up on the next flight from Milwaukee which, according to the arrivals board, was still over three hours away, did not seem practical.

'I'm so out of here,' Liffey finally decided, texting her aunt with instructions to meet her at their hotel. 'I'd rather park myself in the hotel lobby and watch dancers arrive than wait around here.' She hoped her aunt had managed to get on the right plane and was not going to end up somewhere in Alaska or Canada. For all she knew, Aunt Jean might not turn up at all.

Liffey had looked forward to this Seattle Feis for a long time. It would be very exciting doing her steps wearing a Halloween costume instead of her drab, ugly school dress–especially the werewolf costume her mother's cousin, Laura, had surprised her with shortly before she and her father left Pittsburgh after their annual 'visit the relatives' trip. Until the unexpected wolf costume turned up, Liffey had planned to wear a French Apache dancer outfit with a little black mask.

"Your mother would have so loved this werewolf costume," Cousin Laura had told Liffey. "We used to go trick-or-treating together and her costumes were always the best. She taught herself how to sew so she could design and make them all by herself. She wanted to have complete artistic control at the age of twelve! I have no such talent, so I had this costume made for you by a seamstress who advertised at the Irish Heritage Center. I hope you like it. Doesn't it look life-like?"

Liffey had to agree that it looked like a real wolf without its skeletal system and nothing like the stereotyped Hollywood kind of wolf man. The face mask fit snugly, almost like real skin, and Liffey counted 42 plastic teeth protruding from the mouth made with brown rubber gums. The one-piece body suit had two layers of faux fur that looked like it could have easily belonged to a real gray wolf. The top layer of fur was long and coarse. The underfur was shorter and softer.

Liffey shivered. 'This costume seems almost too real. It's kind of creepy, but I guess that's the point.' Liffey decided she would google 'wolves' when her father deposited her at the Pittsburgh Airport for her flight to Seattle. Maybe she could howl or growl at the black haired twins if they turned up in Seattle.

After reading about wolves for over an hour, Liffey discovered that her werewolf costume was so accurate it could have been taken directly off the body of a wolf. Even the paws were right. There were five toes on each forefoot and four toes on the hind feet. Liffey learned that wolves walked on their toes and that they had scent glands between their toes that left chemical markers along the paths they walked so their pack could easily find them if they got separated.

The bushy tail felt like real fur, and Liffey accidentally discovered that if she pressed the center of the black nose, the large, pointy ears attached to the facial mask wiggled back and forth from side to side just like the ears of real wolves when they listen for sounds. 'This is an amazing Halloween costume,' Liffey thought. 'I will have to get Aunt Jean to take a picture of me in it to send to Laura with my thank you note.'

***

Liffey left the terminal and immediately found a taxi. Soon she saw the tall Seattle Space Needle peeking through cracks between even taller buildings in downtown Seattle. Mount Rainier framed the distant horizon like a perfect picture post card.

As if on cue, the white-haired taxi driver launched into his tourist presentation: "First time in Seattle, miss?"

"Yes sir, it is." Liffey braced herself.

"Well, look straight ahead. You can see the Space Needle now. Make sure you take the time to go up in it. Best views of Mount Rainier are from up there."

Liffey was very used to listening to the long, boring, endless history lectures given by her father whenever they traveled together and had resigned herself now to a local history lecture from this cab driver. But he was apparently already done talking and Liffey relaxed.

When she arrived at the multi-storied feis hotel, she found a comfortable lobby chair and settled into it with her *Anne of Green Gables* book. It would be at least three hours yet until her aunt arrived from Milwaukee.

***

A stir in the lobby shocked Liffey out of a sound sleep. A slight, black haired girl, who appeared to be around Liffey's age, was brushing tears away from her cheeks. A loud desk clerk was telling the girl and everyone else within ear range, that she could not check into this hotel without an adult. Even if she *had* come all the way from Ireland. He was very sorry, but that was the way it was here in Seattle.

"I don't think so," Liffey muttered, jumping quickly out of her chair and running over to the distraught girl with a big welcoming hug.

"Hey! Here you are! I guess I fell asleep over in the corner."

Liffey turned to the obnoxious desk clerk and said, "She's with me and my Aunt Jean who is arriving from Milwaukee anytime now. We have a suite on the 18th floor. My name is Liffey Rivers, and my cousin did not have the opportunity to explain to you that she is staying here at your friendly hotel with the Rivers family."

As they walked away from the desk, arm in arm, Liffey asked, "Where in Ireland do you come from?"

"Ossory," the grateful girl answered.

"Where is Ossory?" Liffey asked.

Liffey did not think that this question was out of line. People were always asking you where you came from and this dancer from Ireland had already told her she was from Ossory. However, Liffey could see that this fragile looking girl was visibly shaken now.

"It doesn't matter," Liffey said quickly. "I wouldn't know where it was on a map anyway. I've never been to Ireland but my father keeps promising to take me there. My mother was a McDermott from Sligo."

"What's your name then?" Liffey continued, hoping this inquiry was not going to cause a problem.

The pallid, obviously distressed girl smiled. "My name is Kathleen," she answered. "Thank you very much for all your help. I will pay my own way here though. I do not need any charity. I brought plenty of money."

"My mother wanted very much to come over with me but something unexpected," Kathleen hesitated, "came over her." Her voice trailed off.

'That's an odd way of telling someone your mother did not come along to the States with you,' thought Liffey, wanting to push for more details but sensing this would make Kathleen even more uncomfortable than she already was.

"Well not to worry. You can stay with me and my Aunt Jean for as long as you like. To be honest, I would love to have your company. I don't know anyone here. My aunt means well, but she totally drives me crazy. She talks constantly and is always going on about eating lettuce salads and goes way overboard about everything."

"She came to a feis last spring and cheered for me by name in the middle of the crowd like a total head case. But she is very good-hearted and would do anything for you. You'll like her. Just prepare yourself. And no way are you going to pay! My aunt reserved a suite with three bedrooms for only the two of us. Maybe she knew you were coming!"

Kathleen perked up considerably. "Do you think we might have a view of Mount Rainier or the Space Needle?"

"I hope so," Liffey replied. "We definitely have to go up in the Space Needle after we dance."

Liffey was delighted that this Seattle Halloween Feis suddenly included an unexpected friend. "How old are you, Kathleen? I'm eleven but I like to think I seem a bit older."

A fearful look flashed across Kathleen's lovely face and Liffey regretted now that she had revealed her own age. 'Maybe Kathleen would not want to stay with an eleven-year-old girl at this feis?'

"I'm guessing you're thirteen?" said Liffey.

"That's about right," Kathleen grinned, finally at ease. Before Liffey could decide whether or not she should ask Kathleen any more personal questions or just back off, a high pitched voice sounded from the entrance to the hotel lobby: "Liffey, darling! Liffey, I'm over here!"

Liffey gave Kathleen a little tap on the shoulder and said, "Get ready. It's show time."

Aunt Jean was struggling with her luggage as Liffey and Kathleen rushed to her side to help. "Aunt Jean, this is

Kathleen…" Liffey paused. "You know, I forgot to ask you what your last name is? I mean your surname?"

The little trace of color that had been in Kathleen's face faded away and she stammered, "My last name is Allta. I mean Altan." Liffey was beginning to be a bit concerned about her new friend. 'She gets totally spooked if you ask her anything about herself and how can she not be sure of what her own last name is?'

Aunt Jean gushed, "Well how nice to meet you, dear. I can tell you have an Irish accent. I do hope that means you have come over for the feis from Ireland? I love making new acquaintances. It broadens one's horizons."

"That's very true," Liffey interrupted. "Aunt Jean, at the last minute, Kathleen's mother could not come here to Seattle with her so she came over alone. May she stay with us, please?"

Aunt Jean was thrilled by this prospect. "Of course! You *must* stay with us, Kathleen. I insist. You can tell us all about 'The Emerald Isle' and then all three of us will climb to the summit of Mount Rainier together the day after the feis. It will be glorious!"

Liffey gave Kathleen, an 'I warned you' look and said, "I don't think it's that kind of mountain, Aunt Jean. It's not an easy climb and you need all kinds of special equipment and clothing. I watched a really interesting documentary about climbing Mount Rainier which showed that even very experienced mountain climbers often have trouble getting up and down Mount Rainier. And they don't always make it all the way up to the top either."

"Well do not worry about the proper equipment and clothing, Liffey, darling, I will take care of everything. We will rent our climbing boots and equipment at one of those boutiques where they give you wonderful trail mixes to nibble on as you make your way up the mountain. I have four lovely ski sweaters packed and six pair of warm socks. We shall begin our climb first thing Monday morning after the two of you are all rested up from your dancing."

"How long can you stay here in the States with us, Kathleen? We may have to camp overnight several times on the way up the mountain."

Liffey could tell that Kathleen seemed to be worried about this invitation to go mountain climbing.

"Well, I'm not really sure, miss. My ticket date can be changed with a small penalty fee, I think, but if something unexpected happens, I may have to go back immediately."

'There she goes with the 'unexpected' thing again,' Liffey thought. Before Liffey could think of anything to say, Aunt Jean said: "Well then, it's all settled. If something unexpected occurs, you can certainly return immediately to Ireland and I will pay your ticket change penalty. If nothing unexpected comes up, the three of us will conquer Mount Rainier. I have never climbed a mountain before."

'That's an understatement,' thought Liffey. As far as Liffey knew, her Aunt Jean had never even taken a long hike, let alone camped out. 'If Daddy invited her to come along with us on a camping trip she just laughed at us like we were crazy and now a dangerous, snowy mountain climb with a few overnights on treacherous slopes is no big deal?' Liffey shuddered. She would have to think of something fast and figure out she could talk her aunt out of this crazy idea.

10

"Aunt Jean, maybe we should get settled in. Kathleen must have some serious jet lag."

"Actually, I managed to get six hours sleep on the plane, and I feel pretty good," Kathleen said. Liffey was happy to see that her new friend had apparently cheered up.

"In that case, let us bring these bags upstairs and then we will go and find a wonderful restaurant with some Seattle coffee and fresh salmon. We will unpack after we've eaten," Aunt Jean declared in her itinerary planning voice.

Kathleen eagerly agreed. Recently, she was ravenous most of the time. Her mother told her it was a sign that things were going to start happening soon and she should begin preparing herself.

On the plane she had eaten two full dinners. When she had accidentally spilled water over her dessert, a flight attendant replaced it with a new tray of food. She quickly devoured the entire second meal and moved on to the three sliced ham and cheese sandwiches her mother had packed. Now she was ready to eat again.

Fish sounded wonderful. Maybe it would be heaps of fresh salmon, warm and raw at room temperature. Suddenly Kathleen noticed saliva running out of the corner of her mouth and down her cheek. She was horrified. 'Am I drooling thinking about raw fish?' she thought anxiously. 'How disgusting.'

"Please, not yet!" she prayed.

***

Following a sumptuous dinner of lobster mashed potatoes and grilled salmon, seated at a table overlooking the Seattle Ship Canal, Aunt Jean announced that it was time for them to return to the hotel to "mentally prepare themselves for the feis tomorrow."

Kathleen had said that she would be dancing at the Open Championship level for the very first time. Liffey had never even *talked* to an Irish dancer at this highest level of competitive Irish dance before, and was determined to help Kathleen do her best.

Liffey was not particularly interested in her own competitions tomorrow. She had already qualified in all of her Advanced Beginner steps to dance at the Novice level. But since no one had yet taught her the more complex Novice steps, she went to competitions and danced just to keep up her competitive edge. Later this fall, after the Thanksgiving holiday, her father promised Liffey that he would look into why she was not being taught higher level steps. In the meantime, Liffey was excited and preoccupied about dancing in her life-like Halloween werewolf costume tomorrow.

✳✳✳

"I'm going to show you my costume, Kathleen. Aunt Jean, please do **not** tell her what it is! I want it to be a surprise."

"I won't peek," Kathleen promised.

It took Liffey almost five minutes to get herself into the snug fitting werewolf costume. When she finally felt her mouth placed properly in the mask, she emerged from her room on all fours, growling.

Aunt Jean was delighted and clapped her hands and laughed.

Kathleen let out a loud shriek and passed out.

Liffey jumped to her feet and ran over to Kathleen who looked peaceful and comfortable sprawled out on the thick green carpeting. Aunt Jean was very distraught and said, "What should we *do*, Liffey? Your werewolf costume must have frightened Kathleen." Sometimes Liffey wished her aunt would just take charge. After all, she was supposed to be the adult here.

"Please get a cold wash cloth, Aunt Jean."

"How do I get it to be cold, Liffey?"

'This is totally pitiful,' Liffey thought, 'Aunt Jean really doesn't know what I mean.'

"Just run it under cold water in the bathroom sink, Aunt Jean," Liffey said, trying not to sound too annoyed.

"Oh yes, of course!" Aunt Jean sprinted down the short hallway leading to the bathroom.

Liffey pulled off her wolf head and paw gloves and felt Kathleen's wrist for a pulse. It was strong and steady, neither racing nor slow. Aunt Jean returned quickly and handed her a cold, wet wash cloth which Liffey applied to Kathleen's forehead. This revived Kathleen immediately.

"Why am I lying on the floor? What happened?" she asked.

"You fainted, dear, and Liffey has revived you," Aunt Jean said matter-of-factly. "Now let's get you into bed so you can function tomorrow. One cannot just ignore jet lag you know. It always catches up with you eventually." Liffey agreed and helped Kathleen up from the floor.

Kathleen seemed to be sleepwalking on the way to her bedroom. Liffey gently guided her over to a large queen size bed. Aunt Jean raced past them and pulled down the thin covers.

"There should be extra blankets in the hall closet, Liffey. I'll go look." Liffey was relieved that her aunt had finally begun to help. Kathleen was already asleep.

"Thanks, Aunt Jean. I'll pull Kathleen's nylon socks off so her feet don't sweat all night."

Liffey began to pull down the left sock but stepped back when she got a whiff of wet dog fur. It reminded her of how her dog Max smelled after he came inside from the rain or snow.

She did not want Aunt Jean to pick up the scent so she followed her out into the hall. "Aunt Jean, could you please get a glass of cold water from the kitchen so we can leave it for Kathleen on her bed stand?"

"Good idea, Liffey, darling," Aunt Jean said in her pep assembly voice. She handed Liffey a fluffy blue quilt and started back down the hall for a glass of ice water. Liffey smiled. Aunt Jean had actually stepped up to the plate.

Liffey went back into the bedroom and quickly pulled Kathleen's sock all the way off the left foot.

"Ew!" Liffey stepped back.

Kathleen's toes were covered with thick, dark fur which appeared to be creeping up to the top of her foot. She pulled the right sock off and discovered even more fur on this foot. 'What in the world is going on with Kathleen's feet?' Liffey worried, as she hurriedly yanked the blankets up and over Kathleen's legs before Aunt Jean returned to the room.

Liffey recalled that earlier that evening after dinner, when they were returning to their rental car in the parking lot, a Golden Retriever on a leash had barked ferociously at Kathleen, lunging at her like she was some kind of mortal enemy. The dog's owner was horrified and assured the three of them that he had no idea why his good-natured dog was behaving so out of character. Liffey had noticed then that Kathleen did not react at all. It was almost like she was not surprised that a supposedly gentle dog was behaving in such a menacing way towards her.

'Kathleen has got to know something seriously weird is going on with her feet. I hope it's not contagious,' thought Liffey with an involuntary twitch.

Liffey left Kathleen to say good night to her aunt who was already dozing in the bedroom across the hall. Then she moved the furniture around in the large living room sitting area so she could practice her jig and think. It was always easier to think more clearly when she was dancing. The jig was her best step and she hoped that her Irish dance teacher would get around to teaching her a Novice one soon so she could have a real shot at getting her first 'First Place' and be eligible for a solo dress.

From the moment Liffey had seen the advanced dancers from her school wearing their colorful solo dresses at a performance, she could think of little else. Every day she imagined herself wearing one of those beautiful dresses and people whispering as she passed by that they had never seen anything like it.

Liffey was concerned now, however, about how she was going to get Kathleen's thick, furry feet into her hard shoes and ghillies tomorrow morning. Kathleen's dance shoes were placed neatly underneath a black and gold pirate costume hanging in the closet and Liffey could tell that they were not going to go on easily, if at all. Especially if Kathleen grew any more hair on her feet over night.

15

Instead of practicing her jig, Liffey plopped down on the couch, found her phone in her backpack and began to search online for 'wolves in Ireland.' She had done some research in the airport in Pittsburgh about wolves in general while she waited for her plane to Seattle, but not specifically about wolves living in Ireland. Kathleen had screamed and fainted when Liffey had crawled out of her room dressed like a werewolf. 'What was it that had unnerved Kathleen so much that she had passed out?'

Liffey discovered that wolves in Ireland had been extinct for centuries. 'That might explain why Kathleen had been so totally freaked out. She's probably never seen a real wolf and my costume looks like the real thing.' Next, Liffey searched 'werewolves in Ireland.'

The first heading that came up was: **Werewolves of Ossory**. A deep chill flowed up and down Liffey's back like ice water. 'Isn't Ossory the place where Kathleen told me she came from in Ireland?'

Liffey jumped up from the couch and crept softly into Kathleen's room for another look. In the shadows, Liffey could see that Kathleen was sound asleep gripping the top blanket on her bed with two hairy--paws. Her face was becoming distorted as well and it seemed to be slowly changing into the head of what appeared to be a wolf. Liffey could hardly believe her eyes.

She ran back to the sitting room to use her inhaler and collect her thoughts. 'There is no way this can really be happening,' Liffey concluded. 'I must be asleep and this is a dream brought on by my new werewolf costume.' She pinched her face and it hurt. She was not dreaming.

'What am I going to do with Aunt Jean?' Liffey thought frantically. 'She freaks out at the petting zoo if a baby animal makes eye contact with her from the inside of its cage. I need to get a grip on this unexpected turn of events. Unexpected! That was the word Kathleen had used to explain why her mother could not accompany her to Seattle! "Something unexpected came over her," is how Kathleen had put it.'

'Unexpected is a strange way to put it if Kathleen's mother has actually turned into a wolf. I will have to tell Aunt Jean tomorrow that Kathleen is wearing a werewolf costume like me for the Halloween Feis if the fur keeps spreading and her head keeps changing.'

Right now, Liffey knew it was important to search for more information about Ossory and the werewolves that supposedly came from there. She was shocked to find out that in sixth century Ireland, an abbot called Saint Natalis had become very annoyed with a clan named Allta in County Meath, so he put a terrible curse on the family.

Liffey felt the room spin. Kathleen had told her that 'Allta' was her family's last name before she freaked out and suddenly changed it to 'Altan.'

Liffey forced herself to read on. Two members of this unfortunate extended family had to take the form of a wolf in seven year shifts. After seven years, they could return to the clan, shed their wolf skins and another two clan members would take their place. And on and on, for eternity. Was it possible that this curse could still be in effect?

'I would call Daddy about this for some advice but he would immediately have me sent off to a psych ward,'

17

Liffey thought, searching online again for the definition of the word 'Allta.' Immediately after Kathleen had told Liffey 'Allta' was her name, she had looked very troubled, like she had said something wrong. Then she had quickly changed her surname to 'Altan.'

The online Irish-English dictionary definition of the word 'Allta' was: ***Adjective (animals) wild.***

Liffey could scarcely breathe now and gave herself one more puff from her emergency inhaler. 'I am so cursed here myself,' she thought, clenching her fists. 'How am I supposed to maintain some kind of composure?'

'What am I going to do? If I tell Aunt Jean, she will panic and call the police. If the police come and take Kathleen, it will be like that ET movie Daddy rented and she will be quarantined somewhere to be experimented on. Maybe she'll just bark a bit like Max and whine when she's hungry. I think I can deal with that,' Liffey decided.

Then a completely horrifying thought penetrated Liffey's already overloaded brain circuitry: 'Were she and her Aunt Jean **safe**? What if Kathleen was turning into a man-eating wolf?'

Thoughts were swirling around in Liffey's head like a dust storm. 'What kind of saint puts a curse on a family anyway? Aren't saints supposed to be nice?'

If the gentle Kathleen actually *was* turning into a man-eating werewolf in the next room, there was little time to prepare for what might be about to take place.

Liffey drew in a deep breath and tiptoed down the hallway towards Kathleen's bedroom. Even though she suspected that Kathleen must know what was happening to her by now because of her peculiar behavior earlier in the

18

day, it was obvious that she was frightened and needed a friend. 'Who wouldn't be scared to death?' thought Liffey as she sucked in one more gulp of oxygen and quietly turned the door knob.

Through the partially open door, Liffey could hear loud snoring. It reminded her of Max the Magnificent, her little white terrier. This familiar breathing noise comforted her somewhat. 'I suppose a werewolf is really just a big dog.'

It was very hard to even imagine that this painfully shy Kathleen could be turning into a ferocious beast that might actually attack her. 'Maybe I better call room service and get some meat up here,' Liffey thought nervously.

Under the soft ceiling night lights, she could see that Kathleen's head no longer resembled the pretty girl she had met earlier today in the hotel lobby. Lying on her side, Kathleen looked more like the wolf in Little Red Riding Hood all tucked up in bed underneath a pile of blankets, pretending to be Red Riding Hood's grandmother.

Liffey closed the door and tiptoed back into the living room to call room service. Eventually, she would have to figure out something to tell Aunt Jean about the odd meat order she was about to place.

Aunt Jean was always much easier than her father to explain things away to because her aunt's attention span was limited and she rarely discussed any topic for more than thirty seconds.

Attorney Robert Rivers, at the other extreme, never stopped discussing things if he thought something Liffey said or did was not quite right and would interrogate her endlessly about the 'facts.' One thing Liffey knew for certain was that when she became an adult, she was never going to become a boring lawyer like her father.

"I would like ten uncooked sirloin steaks, please," Liffey said into the phone to the startled order-taker with as much false bravado as she could manage to muster up. There was a long pause.

"Do you mean you want them raw and bloody?"

"Yes, I guess so," Liffey replied. There was another long pause.

"What would you like to have with those steaks? Fries or baked potato?"

"Just the steaks, please. I'm on a special diet."

"O.K. then. It'll be about twenty minutes. I will have to unthaw them first."

Liffey hung up the phone and sighed. It was hard not having a mother to talk to during emergency situations like this. Aunt Jean did her best but she was just not cut out to be maternal, and talking to her father was like voluntarily putting herself on the witness stand during a trial to be cross examined by the prosecutor.

She thought again about the lovely lady she had met earlier today on the plane who wore the diamond 'M' necklace and had been so easy to talk with. 'Why did I forget to ask her for her name?' Liffey was sure that the diamond 'M' lady would know what to do now.

Once again, Liffey quietly crept down the hall past Aunt Jean's room where her aunt's snoring was even louder than Kathleen's. "This place sounds like a zoo," Liffey muttered.

Gathering up every bit of courage she could find, Liffey forced herself to completely open the door so she could better observe Kathleen's terrifying transformation in progress. It was pitch dark inside. The overhead night lights were no longer casting soft shadows on the walls. Had Kathleen turned off the lights? Some kind of threatening tension in the air warned Liffey to stop immediately and not to continue into the room. Her heart was racing as she stepped back into the hallway and shut the door behind her.

Before she could think of a safe way to reconnect with Kathleen, there was a tap on the outside door and a deep voice called out: "Room Service!"

Liffey rushed to open the door before Aunt Jean woke up. She was not yet ready to discuss this werewolf situation with anyone.

When the delivery man pushed a small table on wheels past her into the suite, Liffey was dismayed to see a white linen table cloth and a fancy centerpiece of freshly cut flowers. All she had ordered was a plate of raw meat.

A stack of ten blue plates, linen napkins and cutlery surrounded a large serving platter heaped high with ten raw sirloin steaks. The elderly delivery man looked uneasy as Liffey signed for the steaks. She had forgotten that she was still wearing her werewolf costume except for the head and paws.

"Do your parents know that you have ordered all this raw meat, young lady?"

"It's for our pet, Kat."

"All this meat is for a cat?"

"No, sir. It's for a dog named Kat." Liffey reached into her wolf costume sleeve and pulled out a ten dollar bill. He appeared to be grateful that Liffey knew a tip was expected.

"Well your dog is one lucky animal, miss. I hope she enjoys her stay with us."

"I'm sure she will. Thanks very much. Good night."

Liffey leaned against the closed door for support. It was time to stop sneaking around. 'This time, I will knock on Kathleen's door and see what answers.'

Liffey recalled that in the Werewolves of Ossory legend, the wolves were not running around trying to turn everyone into other werewolves or eating people. They talked like human beings who happened to be trapped in wolf skins. Liffey clearly remembered reading about a man-wolf who spoke with a priest in a dense forest about helping his sick wife that he called a wolfen.

'That wolf talked and reasoned just like a man.' Why should she assume that Kathleen was going to turn into a wolf that would be dangerous? The Werewolves of Ossory were not like most of the werewolves Liffey had researched online. They were victims of a vicious curse that apparently no one had yet figured out how to remove.

It suddenly occurred to Liffey that Kathleen might have come all the way over from Ireland to this Halloween Feis just so she would still be able to dance if she started turning into a wolf.

Her mother had most probably already begun to change into a werewolf and was not able to come to Seattle.

Kathleen had told her that she was going to compete for the first time at the Open Championship level at this feis. Liffey knew that when Kathleen turned into a werewolf, it might be seven long years before she would return to her real self again.

'Poor Kathleen. She took a big chance coming here all the way from Ireland and now the worst is happening and she's all alone.'

Liffey walked to Kathleen's bedroom door and knocked twice. There was no answer. She knocked again. "Kathleen, I think I know what's happening to you. Don't be afraid. May I come in? I have some food for you. It's raw meat."

A long, piercing howl sounded from the room. "Is that a yes?" Liffey asked anxiously. She pushed the door open a crack but remained in the hall until she could figure out what Kathleen was going to do.

"Kathleen, if you want something to eat please come out here with me and we will have a midnight snack."

Liffey pushed the food cart over to the dining room table, tried not to gag looking at the pile of raw meat and sat down. She could hear Kathleen whining like every dog does when it smells dinner and is anxious to eat. Minutes passed and the whining grew louder, almost frantic. Liffey closed her eyes and prayed when she heard sniffing sounds moving slowly towards her.

"Here you are, Liffey! Whatever happened to me? I must have fainted and you put me to bed? Thanks very much. I'm so hungry! May I please have a little piece of your midnight snack?"

Liffey opened her eyes and smiled at the chatty gray wolf which was sitting directly across from her at the table holding a raw, sixteen ounce steak in each of its two front paws.

From start to finish, Liffey estimated it had taken her new werewolf friend less than ten minutes to devour the entire pile of sixteen ounce raw steaks that room service had delivered.

'That's like almost one steak a minute. It's obvious that poor Kathleen has not realized yet that she has totally morphed into a real wolf,' thought Liffey. 'She's eating raw meat like a wild animal while we are chatting normally about tomorrow and how she hopes she hits all of her clicks.'

It occurred to Liffey that Kathleen's dancing shoes were going to be a big problem. 'How in the world is she going to squeeze her feet or paws or whatever wolves call their feet, into her hard shoes and ghillies? I will have to measure the back paws tonight and figure out something. I can try the emergency black duct tape I packed and see if I can stuff her paws into her shoes and then tape them on. Maybe I can cut slits in the sides.'

"Liffey, may I please have a bit more to eat?" asked Kathleen hopefully.

This question alarmed Liffey considerably because Kathleen had already consumed ten pounds of sirloin steak. Liffey's research had told her that wolves eat animals like deer and elk, not people. So she and her Aunt Jean were probably not going to be Kathleen's next meal. 'Maybe I can get by with a bowl of cereal before she switches completely to an all meat diet and I have to order in again.'

"Kathleen, I'm afraid that I'm all out of steak. How about some Cheerios?"

"That would be grand, Liffey."

"With, or without sugar?"

"With, please."

Liffey sighed with relief. At least her friend was not yet on an expensive, all meat diet. 'Aunt Jean is bound to notice I have already ordered enough meat to feed a football team.'

She poured a large bowl of cereal and placed it in front of Kathleen who was waiting politely, paws folded on the table, tongue dangling from her white and gray mouth. Then Liffey returned to the small kitchenette to get her own cereal. When she went back to the table, Kathleen was nowhere to be seen.

Liffey heard loud, satisfied slurping at the end of the hall by the suite entrance door. When she investigated, she saw a large tail wagging back and forth and Kathleen on all fours, face pressed down into the bowl of Cheerios.

'Well so much for normal behavior,' thought Liffey. Apparently Kathleen had walked down the hall like a human and then put the bowl down on the floor to dine.

'How in the world is Kathleen going to manage to pull it off tomorrow at the feis? What if she walks around on all fours instead of standing up erect? What if she snarls at the judges or tries to bite the other dancers?'

"We need to talk," said Liffey, patting Kathleen on the head while picking up the empty bowl from the floor.

"Okay, Liffey," Kathleen agreed, "what would you like to talk about?" Liffey sighed. It was going to be a long night.

"To start with," Liffey replied. "How are we going to do tomorrow?"

"Do what, Liffey?" Liffey groaned inwardly.

"Here, let's sit on the couch and get comfortable. Maybe you should start from the beginning, Kathleen, and tell me about this wolf thing. It's almost impossible to believe, you know, and I am really worried about how you are going to do the feis tomorrow without calling attention to the fact that you are actually a real wolf and risk having you picked up and hauled off to some research laboratory or something. How does this werewolf curse situation work in Ireland?"

Liffey continued: "I know about Saint Natalis and how every seven years two members of your Allta clan turn into werewolves and disappear until the next two take their place. What I don't know is where you wolves go to hide out for seven years until the next two turn up and take over for you?"

"I am guessing you wanted to come to this feis and do your first Open Championship competition before you had to disappear for seven years? You'll be twenty years old when this is all over for you. Why can't someone get rid of this terrible curse? It's just not fair."

Kathleen emitted a low growl and Liffey hoped she had not accidentally overstepped the boundaries of normal conversation with a werewolf and stirred things up a bit too much. Kathleen had very long teeth and jaws that looked like they could easily snap off an arm.

"Here, I am going to comb your lovely gray fur while you tell me everything you know about being one of the Werewolves of Ossory," Liffey said. She retrieved a soft hairbrush from her backpack while keeping a close watch on Kathleen, who had begun to yip and yap like a puppy.

Kathleen relaxed and stretched contentedly when Liffey began to gently groom the underfur on her back.

"All I really know about it is that my mum had been trying to tell me for the last six months that unexpected things might start happening to my body that would not be covered in health class at school."

"She said it was nothing to worry about but that when these unexpected things started happening, the two of us would be going on a long vacation to the northwest coast of Ireland and that my father would be relocating somewhere close to us with my brothers and sisters. I didn't pay too much attention because I was very busy working on my school lessons and new Irish dance steps for Open Championship."

"Then, about a week before we were coming over, my mum began to get headaches and said she felt a bit off. Two days before we were to leave, she noticed her ankles were getting hairy and told me about the werewolf curse. She said she had better not risk traveling with me in case she finished changing into one of the Ossory Werewolves before we arrived here in Seattle."

"She said that if it started happening to me after I arrived in the States, I should pretend it was a costume for the Halloween Feis and still have a go at a championship trophy. She never thought that I would not be permitted to check in to a hotel where we had already reserved a room. She gave me an emergency phone number and said to call Father Joseph at once at the Seattle Holy Hill Monastery if things started moving too fast and he would get me safely out of the country and back to Ireland."

Liffey was dumbfounded. "This is so totally unfair, Kathleen! Why can't anyone figure out how to undo the Saint Natalis curse?"

"I don't know, Liffey. It's a deep, dark secret. Every seven years, the entire Allta clan gets really nervous and has to wait for signs to see which family will be sending two of its members off. And the families of the ones already gone off worry constantly about the safe return of their loved ones."

"Will your dad and brothers and sisters be able to visit you?"

"Yes. Mum says that all of us will be staying with the monks and that our neighbors and schools will be told we have moved away temporarily. Of course our Allta relatives will know what's happened to us. This secret has been going on now for so long that somehow it all works out in the end. Mum also told me that the wolf curse is kind of a holy mission and that we should look upon it as a positive thing."

"Kathleen what in the world could be positive and holy about turning into a, no offense, creepy, smelly animal and then having to disappear for seven years?"

Kathleen exhaled loudly. "I will tell you the truth, Liffey. I am going to need your help to get back to Ireland after this feis and I trust you. You have already helped me more than I could ever hope to repay."

"Kathleen…" Liffey cut in.

"No, Liffey, if you were not here with me now, I would be panicked. As things are, I am looking forward to dancing tomorrow. After that, I will get on with it all."

"The truth is, Liffey, the Werewolves of Ossory were appointed by Saint Natalis in the sixth century to guard the most famous relics in Ireland–the bones of Saint Patrick himself which lie deep down in an underground vault in County Donegal."

"I thought that Saint Patrick was supposed to be buried in Northern Ireland?"

"No. Hundreds of years ago, one of our Clan Allta members stole some bones of well known saints from Saint Martin's Church near Kilkenny and Natalis learned of it. These relics had been given to the church by Saint Patrick over a hundred years earlier. Relics used to be worth lots of money and people often stole them from one church to sell to another. Churches competed for pilgrims and pilgrims liked to pray where there were relics of famous saints."

"So if your monastery or church had famous relics, you got more money from people on pilgrimages?"

"Exactly. Saint Natalis put the terrible curse on the Allta Clan and decreed that this clan, which had stolen relics from St. Martin's, would guard the most precious relics in Ireland for all time—the bones of Saint Patrick. Natalis did not want thieves stealing Patrick's remains and then selling them off one by one to the highest bidder. The Werewolves of Ossory want for nothing. We live at the lovely monastery at Saint Patrick's Purgatory in County Donegal, sleeping by day and keeping watch at night."

Before Liffey could reply, Aunt Jean's bedroom door opened abruptly and there was no time to explain the wolf which was curled up at her feet like a big dog, chewing on a sirloin steak bone and telling a remarkable story.

"Liffey, darling! What a sweet dog!"

Liffey was speechless. The moment of truth had arrived. She drew in a deep breath. "Actually, it's not a dog, Aunt

Jean. It's Kathleen practicing for the Halloween Feis. She wants to be completely in character tomorrow."

"You mean like method acting?"

"Yes," Liffey replied, very glad her aunt seemed to be clueless.

"I studied method acting and learned that if you truly believe you are someone, or in your case, Kathleen, 'something' and look deep within yourself for motivation, it works. Groveling on the floor at Liffey's feet tonight is an excellent idea. Nighty night, girls!" Aunt Jean breezed off to her bedroom. Liffey sighed with relief and pulled Kathleen up from the floor.

"We have got to figure out how to get your feet into your dance shoes, and you need to start walking on your two back paws from now on." Kathleen begrudgingly agreed and walked upright down the hall to her bedroom.

After thirty minutes of cutting and duct taping, Liffey was confident Kathleen's paws could be squeezed into her sliced up ghillies and hard shoes as long as the duct tape held up.

"It's 2:00 a.m. You need to sleep, Kathleen. You must be exhausted from all the traveling today, not to mention turning into a werewolf tonight!" Liffey smiled.

"Liffey, I haven't completely turned yet. I know that my feet have a wee bit of hair but…"

'One might say that,' Liffey sighed wearily.

The wakeup call came far too soon. Liffey felt like she had hardly slept at all when she dialed room service and ordered her pre-feis good luck breakfast along with ten pounds of raw hamburger. She hoped Aunt Jean would sleep through breakfast. But even if her aunt did get up and see Kathleen eating the raw hamburger, she would probably think it was just another method acting exercise.

Liffey heard the sound of running water in the shower. 'If Kathleen doesn't notice how hairy she is this morning, she is in serious denial and I will have to do something drastic.'

Liffey could not help thinking about why, after all this time, no one had yet figured out how to remove the curse on the Ossory Werewolves. Enough was enough. Kathleen had told her that thieves used to steal relics of saints and that Saint Natalis wanted Saint Patrick's bones protected for eternity.

Liffey wondered about the possibility of moving Saint Patrick's bones to a safer place to end the curse. A place where modern day electronic security systems and alarms could guard Saint Patrick's remains—not the poor, cursed Allta clan. 'It's already been a zillion years,' thought Liffey, googling 'Saint Patrick's grave' and discovering he was supposed to be buried at a place called Downpatrick, in County Down. 'That's in Northern Ireland, nowhere near any ancient underground vault in Donegal.'

It was time to call Father Joseph at the Holy Hill Monastery. Kathleen had said her mother had told her to contact him if she began changing.

'She's way past changing now, but doesn't seem to get it. Someone is going to have to take her back to Ireland. I hope I can get her through the feis today but after that Father Joseph will have to take over. I am going to ask him

31

if he knows why no one has ever put Saint Patrick's bones in the Downpatrick grave where they're supposed to be. Why should pilgrims keep visiting the wrong burial site century after century?'

Liffey remembered seeing a small brown leather book on Kathleen's bed stand. 'Maybe Father Joseph's phone number is written inside?' She hurried to Kathleen's bedroom and arrived just as Kathleen entered from the shower modestly wrapped up in an extra large bath towel.

"Kathleen, may I look through this little book?"

"Certainly, Liffey. Our pastor found it in an old safe at our parish church. My mother told me to study it when I started changing." Liffey bit her tongue.

Liffey thumbed slowly through the brittle pages of the book. "Kathleen, what is this book about?"

"I don't really know, Liffey. I suppose I will have to start reading it when I start changing."

"I can't take much more of this," Liffey muttered.

"Kathleen, listen up here! Look at your feet. What do you see? Do you see anything unusual down there?"

"Not really," replied Kathleen.

"O.K. Kathleen, drop the towel!"

"I beg your pardon?"

"I said drop the towel Kathleen. You have already turned into an Ossory Werewolf."

Kathleen let the towel fall to the floor, walked over to the full length mirror on the bathroom door and let out a heartbroken whimper.

"See what I mean, Kathleen?" Liffey said gently.

"We need to call Father Joseph and alert him and then we need to get you ready to dance."

32

There was a loud knock on the hallway door. Liffey cringed. She was not ready to face Aunt Jean so early in the morning. Before another knock came, Liffey rushed to the door, pushed last night's dinner cart out into the hall, pressed a five dollar bill into the hands of the surprised breakfast delivery man and signed for the food.

Kathleen had obviously smelled the raw hamburger and was now down on the floor on all fours whining in the background as Liffey closed the door and struggled to pull the room service cart into the suite.

"Stay!" Liffey commanded.

"Please, give me a break here, Kathleen. You can have your meat right now but not on the floor. You must walk down this hallway and sit properly at the table."

Kathleen eagerly complied and walked upright all the way to the dining table. She pulled a chair back and sat down eagerly.

Liffey placed the large platter of raw hamburger in front of the werewolf.

Before Liffey could take a bite of her own pre-feis breakfast bagel loaded with sliced turkey, melted cheese and sliced tomato, an aged, yellowed card fell out of the tiny book she had placed in her bathrobe pocket.

Liffey saw that it had an old drawing of Saint Patrick on the front and barely discernable words written in what appeared to be Latin on the back:

"cum ossuary patrick sub lock adque key itineramus ad drumlin cata pelagi nullus plus testamentum werewolves ossory ero."

'Ossory werewolves' and the word 'drumlin,' which Liffey had learned is a whale shaped hill like the one that Downpatrick Cathedral had been built on, were the only words she could make out.

Liffey googled 'Online Translator: Latin to English.' After a few seconds, the translation appeared. What she read confirmed what she already suspected:

"When the bones of Patrick under lock and key are moved to the drumlin by the sea, no more will the werewolves of Ossory be."

Liffey smiled at Kathleen excitedly. "Kathleen, I am fairly certain that this little card says there will be no need for the Ossory Werewolves to be guarding the bones of Saint Patrick if they are transported to Downpatrick! That should be easy enough to do."

"Liffey, if you are right, I'll be able to compete as myself again very soon and even better, the Allta Clan will be able to lead normal lives!"

"I'm predicting you'll be a major world champion someday, Kathleen," Liffey grinned.

"But first, let's start working on today. You came a long way to dance here in Seattle," Liffey said, trying hard not to rudely stare at the disgusting little pieces of raw hamburger clinging to Kathleen's hairy snout.

Liffey did not tell Kathleen that she had decided not to do her own steps today even though she had already put on her werewolf costume and ordered a pre-feis good luck breakfast. 'It will be hard enough to get Kathleen on and

34

off her own stage before anybody gets suspicious. I'll just tell Aunt Jean and Daddy that I didn't place this morning and that will be the truth.'

After Kathleen's feet had been duct taped into her ghillies, Liffey said, "It's time to get down to your stage. Just do your best and whatever happens will be fine. I am going to contact Father Joseph and pack up your suitcase just in case you will need to leave quickly."

"What about your aunt, Liffey? Shouldn't we wake her up?"

"No, she takes forever getting ready and she's all excited about climbing Mount Rainier tomorrow so that will keep her busy until this afternoon."

✳✳✳

Two werewolves, one of them pulling a large oversized suitcase, walked slowly down the long hotel corridor leading to the championship stage. Liffey walked with Kathleen 'Altan' over to the stage monitor, who checked her name off the roster. A tooth fairy, two fluffy angels and a Peter Pan filed into the championship stage area.

Liffey stood outside of the competition room and kept watch as Kathleen practiced her point-back, rock-rock-rocks and butterflies at the far end of the hallway. 'So far, it's working,' thought Liffey. Everybody thinks she's wearing a great costume.'

A voice announced: "Competition Number Five" and Liffey signaled to Kathleen that it was time. To Liffey's horror, Kathleen started running down the hall on all fours and only stopped when Liffey frantically gestured at her to stand up and walk. Miraculously, it seemed that no one had seen this exhibition. Liffey watched apprehensively as Kathleen boldly walked into the room and took first place in the lineup of what looked to be around fifteen costumed dancers. She noticed that the pink rabbit directly behind Kathleen had stepped back a bit. 'I hope Kathleen doesn't smell too bad.'

Kathleen walked up the stairs and stepped on to the stage like a proper Irish dancer. A hushed murmur went through the audience like a wave and a collective whoop sounded from the astonished spectators when the Slip Jig began and Kathleen jumped at least four feet high and did three perfect butterflies before her ghillied paws returned to the stage floor. The crowd broke into wild applause after the Slip Jig ended.

Kathleen was overcome with emotion and excitement. She bowed to the judges and musician and began to howl with delight. Liffey bit her bottom lip. 'This could be bad,' she thought nervously. The dancer next to Kathleen looked uneasy and backed away with a look of disgust. This caused Kathleen to switch from blissful howls to loud, threatening growls.

Liffey saw the tense audience begin to hurriedly clear out of the competition room and the judges stood up and began slowly backing away from the stage.

Before Liffey was able to make her way through the crowd to help Kathleen, she felt a swish of cold air and a brown hooded monk glided past her. 'It's Father Joseph! He's come for Kathleen.'

With head bowed low, the monk slowly walked up on stage and gently took Kathleen's right paw. He guided her out through huddles of worried people on their phones.

Waiting outside the emergency exit at the end of the hall, Liffey could see a dark car with blacked out windows. She followed behind Father Joseph and the werewolf with Kathleen's oversized suitcase and pressed the little leather book she had found into Father Joseph's free hand.

When the three of them reached the end of the long hallway, Kathleen turned around and hugged Liffey.

"Liffey, I know we will meet up again someday. *Go raibh maith agat, shábháil tú mo shaol!*"

"Liffey, you saved my life. Thank you."

Father Joseph blessed Liffey and shook her hand.

The dark car sped away.

Liffey wiped the tears away from her eyes with the back of her hand and slowly started the long journey back up to her hotel suite where she would have to break the news to her Aunt Jean that there were neither medals nor trophies awarded today at the Seattle Halloween Feis to Liffey Rivers and her new friend, Kathleen Allta.

THE END

THE MYSTERY OF THE MISSING NOVICE

Thirteen-year-old Irish dancer Liffey Rivers strutted her way across the crowded Pittsburgh hotel lobby on an unseasonably warm Friday evening in early November.

Aunt Jean was off parking her car in an attached garage which reminded Liffey of a space shuttle docking station.

All the way to Pennsylvania, Aunt Jean had chattered on endlessly about how arriving at a feis with 'attitude' and a unique signature walk was very important. Liffey thought that most of her aunt's ideas were totally lame but decided to experiment with the aggressive trademark stride her aunt had created for her just to see if anything might actually happen.

Liffey continued strutting through the lobby towards the long registration line, noting that if anyone *had* noticed her unique signature walk, they did not show it.

Irish dancers of every shape and size were swarming around like hundreds of sweat bees at a snow cone stand. Some of the smaller dancers were wearing colorful spiked curlers which matched their track suits. Little feis feet with flashing light up shoes created a disco club atmosphere. Ringtones were going off all around her like canned quiz show music.

'This place is like a bad night at Chuck E Cheese's,' Liffey thought grouchily as she edged forward in the check-in queue at a snail's pace.

Sometimes, Liffey wondered why she did this Irish dancing thing. Ever since her Aunt Jean had become an adult Irish dancer and had started to place in adult Slip Jigs and Treble Jigs *and* Hornpipes, everything seemed surreal and unnatural. Liffey was still stuck in Novice. She was only in Open in one step–her Jig. 'I am not a bad dancer,' she kept reminding herself. 'I am just not yet a great dancer.'

It was not easy going to feiseanna with Aunt Jean. Liffey always had to listen to her aunt's constant chattering about whether or not she was going to place in her adult Irish dancing competitions, and endlessly reassure her aunt that she was sure to win many medals. 'How could you *not* win a medal if it was only you along with two or three other dancers in each competition?'

Aunt Jean agonized anyway and Liffey was getting sick of it. So sick of it that she was even considering quitting Irish dance. She had way more than enough of her own problems competing against twenty-plus dancers each time she stepped onto a Novice stage. And she was tired of playing shrink for her father's peculiar sister. The aunt who had, for some bizarre reason unknown to mankind, decided to become a competitive adult Irish dancer.

'No negatives here, Liffey, just positives,' she reminded herself as the desk clerk handed her their room key cards.

Liffey spun around and this time, decided to walk normally over to the parking garage entrance to the hotel lobby.

'I have got to remember that Aunt Jean is certifiable and must never again take her advice seriously,' Liffey sighed, somewhat embarrassed about her previous lobby strutting. Aunt Jean should arrive soon with their luggage if she could find her way out of the parking garage.

Liffey had packed one small overnight bag and a dress carrier. Aunt Jean had packed two large suitcases with at least twenty outfit changes, along with her own dress carrier, a makeup case and shoe bag.

When Liffey had asked her why she needed so many clothes for a one night hotel stay, her reply was typical Aunt Jean: "Liffey, dear, one must always try to look one's best at these competitive events. One never knows whom one might meet by the pool or in a restaurant or perhaps, just sitting quietly in the lobby reading a newspaper."

'Did Aunt Jean seriously think a touring company of Lord of the Dance was secretly scouting at feiseanna? And like they would seriously be looking for the over forty-year-old dancers if they were?'

"Liffey, darling, Michael Flatley was much older than one would expect a magnificent Irish dancer to be when he became internationally acclaimed," Aunt Jean had said one morning over Cheerios.

Liffey tried to explain to her aunt that Michael Flatley had danced for a million years before he became famous and that she had only been an adult Irish dancer for a few months, but Aunt Jean did not get the point. "Age means *nothing*, Liffey, nothing at all unless one permits it to get in one's way."

Liffey held her breath and tried hard not to laugh when her aunt reached the conclusion of her speech. "So one must always be prepared for fame and fortune, Liffey. Prepared and ready to take that next important step up the ladder of success."

While Liffey waited for her aunt to make her celebrity guest appearance from the parking garage, she could not help but notice a small group of five noisy little girls who looked to be about eight or nine years old, practicing their jigs in their socks.

They appeared to be good friends and were laughing so hard that most of the time they could not remember their steps. This made them laugh even harder until they collapsed together into a heap on the tiled lobby floor.

Their hilarity reminded Liffey of her best friend Sinead in County Sligo and how much she wanted to get back to Ireland to visit her again. It had been a little over two months since the Beltra Feis. Two long months of living in what seemed like a dream.

Presently, Liffey was stuck living with Aunt Jean until "things returned to normal," as her father optimistically put it when he called her each night from Ireland. The only bright spot was that Robert Rivers had decided that Liffey did not have to be imprisoned any longer at the local junior high school. No more Principal Godzilla's squeaky shoes patrolling the hallways! Aunt Jean was home schooling Liffey now and it was like being taught by the president of the 'Let's Cut School Today Club.'

Liffey had to admit Aunt Jean was a great, if somewhat peculiar, teacher. They rarely did any of the assignments in the textbooks her father had ordered. Instead, they took

41

field trips to all kinds of interesting places like skin care clinics. These clinics were really expensive makeup and facial salons. Aunt Jean insisted that since skin was their main focus, their trips counted as Science units.

"The skin on human beings is the largest of our body organs," Aunt Jean had explained like a real teacher.

"If one does not use proper makeup, it could ruin one's skin or perhaps even cause one's skin to detach from the body. Dear Mother Nature has spent millions of years evolving facial mud and makeup." This strange scientific statement surprised Liffey a bit but she was pretty much used to her aunt's weird theories by now.

For physical education they did aerobics classes five times a week. 'Totally legitimate,' Liffey thought.

For Family and Consumer Sciences or what her Aunt Jean called 'Home Economics,' they made and refrigerated three dozen Bakeless chocolate and oatmeal cookies every Monday afternoon.

Liffey suspected that her aunt only knew how to use the top burners on her stove and did not use the oven because she could not figure out how to turn it on and off.

Aunt Jean had explained oven use to Liffey like this: "Baking things in a conventional oven, Liffey, is a higher level of Home Economics. At this moment in time, we are exploring microwave oven and refrigerator technology."

"When you are in high school we shall open up the oven door and experiment with frozen pizzas."

Liffey had long ago stopped worrying about what school curriculum units they were or were not fulfilling each day. Aunt Jean was just too much fun for Liffey to be concerned with what some State Board of Education rule making official might think about their unusual class work. 'If they care so much about your education, then why do they let Godzillas run their schools?'

Aunt Jean's favorite television show was *America's Next Top Model*. They watched new episodes and reruns almost every day. During each show, Aunt Jean would verbally quiz Liffey as to what each of the contestants did best for a Consumer Science unit. The verbal quiz was followed by a written test. Liffey had to answer 'true' or 'false,' or 'yes' or 'no,' to questions on the Top Model exams such as: "Did Mallory accentuate her outfit with the best possible scarf given her choices?"

Once, Aunt Jean had taken Liffey on a two day field trip to the Mall of America in Minnesota where they spent hours analyzing the latest fashions and riding on an indoor rollercoaster. They ate lunch and dinner each day at a Rain Forest Café and Aunt Jean pointed out that these restaurant dining experiences counted towards Biology units because there was a huge aquarium with colorful fish to watch while they ate and also animatronic robots of a gorilla thumping its chest and a trumpeting elephant rearing its animated head.

The friendly wait staff introduced themselves as their safari guides and Aunt Jean got enthused and suggested that perhaps they might go on a real safari soon in Africa to complete their science units.

Aunt Jean called her teaching method 'The School of Life,' and planned to write a bestseller book about Liffey's progress and ultimate success with her system.

Liffey very much appreciated Aunt Jean's kid-friendly teaching methods. She could get up any time she wanted in the morning and watch daytime television with her aunt as part of her cultural enrichment curriculum. Aunt Jean said that watching daytime soap operas and talk shows was like working on Social Studies.

Right now, as she waited for her aunt to find her way out of the parking garage, Liffey could see that the giggling dancers were being collected by their parents. There were apparently three groups of them. Two were probably sisters because one mother collected two of them. The other three were collected by three obviously-not-traveling-together adults in three different directions.

Liffey had observed earlier that two of these little girls looked almost like identical twins but were probably not sisters because they both left with separate parents. 'How could two adorable little girls look so much alike when they are not sisters?' Liffey wondered.

Just then, Aunt Jean breezed in from the attached parking garage like a movie star arriving on the Red Carpet.

"Liffey, darling, it is time for us to eat dinner. We must eat. I am completely famished," Aunt Jean announced, holding her stomach dramatically.

"Sounds like a good plan to me," Liffey said, watching the unfortunate concierge her aunt had lassoed in struggling with the oversized luggage.

"We must both have something light tonight, like lettuce salads so we are not overfed and bogged down before the feis tomorrow morning. None of your pre-feis pasta and meatballs tonight, Liffey, darling," Aunt Jean ordered.

"Very good idea," Liffey agreed, having no intention whatsoever of just eating crunchy rabbit food and totally jinxing her dancing tomorrow. 'Apparently Aunt Jean has never heard of good carbs,' Liffey thought as she reached deep into her backpack to make sure that the lid on the Tupperware ice bucket holding her emergency pre-feis spaghetti and meatballs was not leaking tomato sauce all over her wig.

***

Before they had started out for the Pittsburgh Feis, she had watched Aunt Jean use up all of their Tupperware containers to store mountains of carrots and celery. Liffey had been forced to use her own Tupperware wig carrier for pre-feis emergency cans of Heinz Spaghetti and Meatballs.

Relying upon these canned dinners concerned Liffey somewhat as canned pre-feis dinners were supposed to be used only in cases of extreme emergency. But since there was no hamburger meat in the house to make meatballs and Aunt Jean might smell her preparing a take-along spaghetti and meatballs dinner and then forbid her to bring it with her to the feis, it *was* a serious situation. Especially since Aunt Jean had made it clear she was not going to eat pasta before the feis.

Relieved that her wig was sauce free, Liffey mentally prepared herself to eat the salad her Aunt was going to force feed her at dinner. She would eat the spaghetti and meatballs later in their room when Aunt Jean fell asleep and started snoring.

***

Aunt Jean was sputtering like an outboard motor boat engine that would not catch and start.

45

Liffey was propped up fully dressed with her pink stuffed monkey, Mrs. Pooh, inside the dry bathtub slowly eating her pre-feis cold spaghetti and in this case, thanks to Max, one meatball dinner.

She did not dare use the microwave in their room to heat it up because even though Aunt Jean was snoring twice as loudly as Max the Magnificent, who was now gurgling peacefully under Liffey's feet, Aunt Jean was actually a very light sleeper. A beeping microwave would definitely wake her aunt up and if Liffey got out of the bathtub now, she would probably wake Max up as well.

Max had refused to get out of the car when they arrived at the hotel, baring his teeth and growling when Liffey and her aunt had tried to wake him up on the back seat. Max loved road trips. He never wanted to get out of the car. Now he was fast asleep again in the tub and Liffey could tell he was out for the night. Three spaghetti noodles hung from his whiskers and there was no trace of the meatballs he had managed to get at before they reached Liffey's mouth.

Liffey continued to slowly pick at her own dinner even though she was not hungry and there was only one meatball left. She swallowed each noodle separately, holding it up like she imagined how a fish would eat a worm, nibbling at most of the noodle and then quickly sucking in the last little bit.

She knew she ought to stop the spaghetti games and get back to reading War and Peace which was just outside the bathtub on the tiled floor. But with all the loud snoring coming at her from the bedroom and Max making loud slobbering noises, her brain could not relax enough to take

46

another stab at that fat, endless book. It was just too noisy to even think here let alone try to read an impossible book.

Liffey wondered if anyone had actually ever read War and Peace in the last hundred years or if it had always been just one of those 'big points books' on school contest reading lists. Still, she was determined to get through this book because somehow she knew that when she actually did manage to read the very last page, it would not be long before she would get a first place in her Hornpipe. First, read War and Peace. Then get the first place. It was all tied together in some mysterious way.

The last page! 'Why haven't I thought of this before?' Liffey eagerly reached for Tolstoy's epic book. She would read *only* the last page–just to see what would happen. Nothing ventured, nothing gained. If she could not trick fate, then so be it. At least she could try. It would save her many monotonous hours of trying to figure out who was who and what was going on in this long, boring book. And if it worked, she would know tomorrow morning shortly after she did her Hornpipe.

If it did not work, she would have to get back to reading the book. It was totally worth trying. She picked up War and Peace for what she hoped would be the final time and forced herself to read the last page.

Liffey yawned. She was finally getting sleepy. Earlier that night, she and her aunt had eaten lettuce salads that cost twenty-five dollars each at a restaurant in the hotel called 'The Lettuce Leaf.' Over huge piles of greens, Liffey listened politely to her aunt obsessing about tomorrow's feis and how micronutrients and therapeutic herbs could completely change your life.

This constant duty of being her Aunt Jean's sounding board and shrink had surprisingly helped Liffey to control her own jittery nerves and doubts. Even though she was still seriously considering quitting Irish dance, the prospect of traveling to faraway feiseanna with her aunt and the fact that she was fairly certain that her own dancing was finally improving, kept Liffey from making any drastic decisions.

***

When Liffey woke up in the hard, cold bathtub it was already 7:00 a.m. She felt stiff but at least she had gotten some sleep. She wanted to eat the pre-feis turkey, cheese, and sliced tomato-on-a-bagel breakfast she had brought along with her before her aunt got out of bed and started force feeding her bunny food again.

Aunt Jean was so unpredictable. Just a few weeks ago she had insisted that they eat a Mars Bar for breakfast each morning because she had read about Arctic explorers in the 1950's who "lived on just one Mars Bar a day and remained perfectly healthy in the midst of all the ice and snow."

There was absolutely no doubt about it. Aunt Jean was completely nuts.

Liffey looked disgustedly at the large jar of smashed cucumber and avocado her aunt had pounded into a mucky paste to 'soothe' her face between today's soft shoe and hard shoe competitions. It was sitting in a bowl next to the microwave waiting to be warmed up. Liffey tried not to look at the goop while she warmed up her own good luck breakfast. Aunt Jean must have been in a deep REM cycle because she continued to snore like an elephant with a stuffed up trunk.

***

When Aunt Jean finally did wake up, Liffey spent at least an hour listening to her lecture about why a good night's sleep was vitally important. Liffey resisted the impulse to say to her aunt that she too might have a good night's sleep once in awhile if her snoring auntie would stop the nocturnal honking.

After Aunt Jean had eaten three containers of celery and carrots, Liffey escorted her to the Pittsburgh Steelers Ballroom where the adult Slip Jig stage was located. When they finally reached the area, Liffey saw that, as usual, there was no stage monitor present because there were only three dancers. And since they were adults, they were expected to get on and off the stage by themselves. She gave her aunt a little good luck pat on the back and rushed off before Aunt Jean had time to start whining and agonizing again.

Liffey barely had enough time to make it to her own stage through the crowds which were dense and unfriendly. "Where is the love?" Liffey grumbled, inching her way past anxious mothers who were applying last minute lip gloss to their uncooperative young daughters' mouths.

In spite of all the frustration with Aunt Jean, Liffey found herself dancing confidently this morning and even smiling as she sailed through the Slip Jig steps she had probably done a thousand times by now.

'Someday, I will *have* to get another first place in another step,' she thought, bowing first to the adjudicator, then the fiddle player. 'Mathematically, the odds are totally for it now that I am going to so many feiseanna with Aunt Jean. And there are only fifteen girls in this group.'

Eating the pre-feis spaghetti and meatballs the night before had already paid off. Liffey smiled and stepped happily off the stage. She knew she had danced well. Sometimes, when she *thought* she had done really well, she was very disappointed when she checked the results board. Not today though. She *knew* she had finally nailed her Slip Jig. She actually looked forward to checking the results later.

Liffey was basking in her Slip Jig performance and trying to psych herself up to get to her Reel stage, when she saw the little group of dancers who had been having so much fun in the lobby the night before. This morning they were just as boisterous as they snaked along single file making their way through the dense crowd holding on to the shoulders of the friend in front of them like they were in a Bunny Hop line.

They were still giggling. But there were only four of them this morning. They were wearing their blue school dresses. Liffey looked for a supervising parent, saw none, and then noticed that one of the little look-alike girls was missing from the group.

"Good luck today, ladies," Liffey called out flattening herself against the wall to get by them in the cramped hallway. She fervently hoped a fire alarm would not sound, causing what would have to be a very dangerous exit by so many people crammed into such a small space.

There was also the fact that she was simply not up for another fire drill. Three of them in the last sixty days had been quite enough.

"Where's your friend?" Liffey asked as she squeezed by the linked together gigglers. The girls stopped laughing and stared back blankly at Liffey. "The one who looks just like *you!*" Liffey said, pointing at the shy little girl bringing up the rear in the blue and white school dress.

"Oh, she goes to another school," the little look-alike answered. "She even lives in another state. We only see her at the hotels. And she wears a red dress and she's only in Novice."

Liffey cringed. "Only in Novice," was a phrase that completely described her own dancing situation.

Only in Novice. How advanced were these little girls, anyway? They probably had their own miniature solo dresses already and were only wearing their school dresses now because they were off to do a figure dance together.

Liffey had never been chosen to be on a team.

Maybe it was because she used to growl at some of the snooty dancers in her class, but mostly Liffey thought it was because her ill-tempered dance teacher disliked her for some reason. Even though she had already won her solo dress, she had never been picked for a group figure dance.

Following what Liffey assumed were most likely unintentionally stinging words, the little group continued winding its way through the thick traffic and disappeared into the crushing crowd of animated feis goers.

Liffey watched them for a moment and then turned around, accidentally smacking into the woman directly behind her. "Sorry!" Liffey exclaimed. The woman's eyes

51

were a lovely robin's egg blue but they looked lifeless. Creepy. More like two opaque marbles sitting in eye sockets than actual eyes. Liffey tried not to obviously wince. Except for her eyes and overly tanned skin, the woman appeared to be normal. She had dark brown hair and wore conventional clothing.

"Why don't you watch where you're going little girl?" the creepy woman complained under her breath. 'Definitely troll material,' Liffey thought. Liffey continued down the hallway and looked back once to see if the little girls were still in sight. The old lady had stopped winding her way through the crowd and was directly in back of the girls now and she seemed to be making no attempt to get by them. 'Is she following the little divas?' Liffey shook off her concern momentarily. 'I'll find the girls again right after my Reel to make sure that awful woman is gone,' she decided.

After a ten minute search, Liffey found her Reel stage. As usual, there were over twenty-five girls lining up for the first Novice round in her age group. She really hoped her aunt had gotten a first place by now and would be so elated that she would have rushed back up to their room to put the cucumber slime on her face to 'rest up' until her next round of adult dancing. That way there would be no chance of her showing up to watch the Reel Stage.

While Liffey waited to check in with the stage monitor, she had another flashback to the first time her aunt had seen her dance in Chicago. It had been humiliating. It had been dreadful. It had seemed like the end of the world to Liffey.

Now that Aunt Jean danced herself, she knew better than to violate feis rules by cheering loudly for Liffey when she watched her dance. Even so, Liffey much preferred it when her aunt had better things to do such as applying an avocado mask to refresh her face between soft shoe and hard shoe competitions and was far away from all of her competition stages.

If her aunt did well today, Liffey had decided to ask if they could go somewhere really exotic for their next feis road trip. Like maybe Africa or Alaska.

Liffey knew it was only a matter of time before her aunt became bored with Irish dancing. Aunt Jean, like Max the Magnificent, did not have much of an attention span. She would have to get her aunt to take her to as many far away feiseanna as possible while she was still living with her. It was only a matter of time until her father would make her go back to her regular prison school. Especially when he discovered how little academic work she and Aunt Jean had actually completed.

Liffey knew that Principal Godzilla was waiting for her return, patiently lurking in the dark, dismal middle school corridors until he had her back in his paws again.

***

While Liffey waited for her Reel group to be called, she kept thinking about how the little look-alike dancer had not been with the other girls this morning.

There had been a simple, logical explanation--she did not dance at the Open level like they did. Still, Liffey had an uncomfortable feeling about it. She did not have the prickly pins and needles warnings running up and down her spine which she often experienced if she was headed toward trouble or there was something not right about a situation, but there was a subtle sense of urgency now that she could not seem to shake off--like she was waiting for something bad to happen.

'I am probably just going to totally mess up my Reel but that's nothing new, so why can't I stop thinking about those loud little girls?'

The tall, fidgety black-wigged dancer standing in front of Liffey in line wore a shiny silver solo dress and looked like she was waiting for her head to be chopped off. Her face was a mask of fear and dread when Liffey tapped her on the back and whispered, "Good Luck!" Now that Liffey had her solo dress, she was not as desperate about how she placed. She just did her best. However, the pressure would soon be on again.

The dreaded Hornpipe was waiting for her like a cat ready to pounce on a mouse. Very soon now she would test her hypothesis that fate could actually be tricked. It was heavy stuff. Liffey Rivers may have tapped into a secret of the universe or something that Einstein would have made into an important theory. If she *did* trick fate and got a first in her Hornpipe, who would ever believe that she only got it because she skipped to the end of *War and Peace* and read the last page?

Liffey felt a little shove from behind and realized she needed to be on the Reel stage immediately. She moved quickly into position just as the judge finished writing the competitors' numbers on each of the scoring sheets.

'Like they ever actually write anything useful about your dancing,' Liffey thought impatiently. She was resigned to whatever her Reel fate would be. Her Hornpipe was up next and she would soon know whether or not her theory might be Nobel Prize material. She might even have to take a leave of absence from Irish dancing while she briefed the scientific community throughout the world.

***

The Reel went well. 'At least I looked like a dancer,' Liffey decided after she did her bows and started walking toward her Hornpipe competition which would probably not start for another half an hour. She had just enough time to get to the U-10 stage area and look around to see if the creepy woman who seemed to be shadowing the gigglers was still lurking about.

She spotted the gigglers club immediately. They were hard to miss, even though they had changed from their school dresses into their Barbie-sized, colorful solo dresses. Still no look-alike. There was no sign of the lady with the cloudy marble eyes either.

Liffey approached the little group and asked how things had been going. "Awesome," was their unanimous reply. "Where's your friend?" Liffey inquired again. "Have you seen her at all today?"

"Nope," said the look-alike and then she turned away from Liffey, back to her friends, and exclaimed mockingly: "Oh no! She must be missing!!" This proclamation caused cackles of laughter among the little divas.

Liffey pressed on insistently, "Aren't you worried about her? Like maybe she is sick or something?" This had not seemed to occur to any of the little girls and they did not answer. They stood mute, looking at Liffey like she was a party crasher.

"Why do you keep asking *Caitlin* where *Amanda* is anyway?" one of the divas asked suspiciously. "Why *should* we worry about her?"

Amanda! Liffey finally had a name. "Do you know her *last* name?" Liffey pressed on. Liffey could tell these little girls were not interested in last names. 'These girls probably don't even know their o*wn* last names.' They shrugged indifferently and the pack moved off without so much as a backward glance at Liffey. They were most likely headed out to find an adult to hit up for snack money.

Liffey wondered why not one of their parents was on hand in the U-10 stage area now even though they were obviously little veterans. 'They probably just tell their parents when and where they will meet up with them,' Liffey sighed, thinking how nice it would have been to have had a mother tagging along with her when she had first started competing.

Now it was time to find the Novice Hornpipe stage to meet up with destiny. On the way, Liffey elbowed her way through the ever thickening crowd towards the results wall. Looking down at her 777 competition number, Liffey knew that the same number repeated three times had to be a good omen. When she finally managed to reach the results wall, the number **777** almost flew out at her because it was in the *second* place box of her Slip Jig competition!

Liffey was very surprised because she had not thought about how reading the last page of War and Peace might have affected her other steps today. The highest place she had ever had before in the Slip Jig had been a fifth but Liffey had always been confident that she would eventually get a first place in her Slip Jig and now she was on her way.

It was the Hornpipe she hated and feared. It was never kind to her. If by some miracle she *did* place in it, she was always sixth or lower. Liffey tried to calm herself down as she approached the smiling Hornpipe stage monitor. 'I hope *I* have something to smile about when this is all over,' she thought resignedly.

***

Before she knew it, Liffey heard her feet thudding beneath her with a big punch opening and realized she was doing her Hornpipe effortlessly. She was not even tempted to hold her breath and turn blue to distract the judges from looking at her feet. Her feet seemed to be doing exactly what they were supposed to be doing--a Hornpipe!

She bowed to the judge and musician and began to make her way to her Treble Jig stage in a daze. Before she knew it, her feet were confidently pounding under her once again on a flimsy, wooden stage floor. Could reading the last page of *War and Peace* be like a portal to another dimension? As Liffey made her way back to the results wall, she wondered if she should call a press conference. She felt giddy with the success she was fairly certain she had just earned.

***

"*Why* can't you *ever* watch where you are going, young lady?" Liffey could not believe she had accidentally collided with 'marble eyes' again! Why did she never seem to see this woman? "This is the second time today you have slammed into me! This is not a mosh pit, you know!"

Liffey was tempted to reply: "How would *you* know what it's like in a mosh pit?" right back at this disgruntled, irritable woman, but she had always been taught to be respectful.

"Please excuse me, I'm very sorry," Liffey said politely.

"I am leaving this hotel in exactly 30 minutes and I have had quite enough of this slam dancing!" Mrs. Marble Eyes glowered at Liffey.

Without further comment, the old lady turned around abruptly and continued moving down the hallway towards the exit.

Liffey impulsively decided to follow her. She did not know why she felt she had to follow this lady because she *really* wanted to get to the results wall to see how her Hornpipe and Reel and Treble Jig had turned out. Instead, Liffey slipped in behind the grouchy woman who was dragging her left foot a bit as she walked. Liffey had not noticed this until now.

Liffey watched the limping lady make her way down the hallway and then open the Exit Only door about fifty feet away. After she had counted to twenty, Liffey walked to the door and quietly pushed it open, thinking that this woman was somewhat crippled and would not be moving up the steps quickly.

She flashed back to the staircase in St. Louis. Here she was again. Not technically alone because she was with her Aunt Jean at this feis but her aunt seemed to have disappeared along with the look-alike. Liffey knew she was very much alone at the moment, and that walking into another hotel stairwell unaccompanied like she had done in

58

St. Louis, was stupid and dangerous. She knew better. 'But what can an old lady do to me?'

Liffey slipped into the dimly lit stairwell and began to stealthily sneak up the steps, one by one, carefully listening for footsteps ahead of her. She heard nothing but faraway feis music and tapping feet.

'She must have gone up only one flight of steps,' Liffey decided, when out of nowhere she felt icy cold, bony fingers clamping down on her neck and a hoarse voice asking: "Are you *following* me young lady?"

Liffey could hardly catch her breath. It was obvious that this lady knew she was following her. Liffey resisted the impulse to yank the thin, icy fingers off her neck and flee as she lied: "Following you? No! Of course not! Why would I be following you?"

"That's what I would like to know. Now you listen to me, I may look old and feeble to you, but I am much more resourceful than you could ever imagine and I am warning you right now that if you slam into me or follow me one more time, you will deeply regret it." Little pricking pins and needles began to run up and down Liffey's back.

Liffey was speechless as the old woman released her finger claws and walked away slowly, pulling her crippled left leg up each step by using the stretchy fabric of her baggy slacks. She did not look like a formidable adversary. Dyed brown hair and overly tanned skin masked her true age.

"She's got to be at least one hundred years old," Liffey thought, feeling somewhat foolish as she watched the feeble woman struggling up the stairs with her bad leg. Still, Liffey had the strong feeling that this seemingly harmless

59

old lady was a danger to someone. Liffey hoped it was not herself and quickly left the stairwell before the unpleasant woman had time to turn around to begin another verbal assault.

Even though the results board was straight ahead, Liffey wanted to eat something before she looked at it. She was starving. She had already danced in four competitions and not had anything to eat since 7:00 a.m. She could smell delicious aromas not far away and went after them like Max when he sniffed a can of dog food popping open. 'Poor Max, after I find out how I did, I will take him out for a walk.'

Liffey's nose led her to a taco stand and she bought four. Since this could very well be the last meal she would eat before her life might be forever altered, Liffey munched on the tasty tacos slowly, imagining the looks of "What's *she* doing here?" on the faces of the prizewinner dancers from her school when she confidently stepped up onto their stages to compete against them in the near future.

Liffey polished off the tacos and headed towards her future. She could almost make out the numbers when a familiar voice rang out directly behind her. "Liffey, *darling!* Wherever have you been? I have been looking *everywhere* for you!"

Liffey cringed. Aunt Jean must have used her internal feis radar to locate her. Liffey did not know how she did it. One time, hiding from her aunt in a bathroom, Aunt Jean sailed into the huge tiled floor ladies room and immediately knocked on the door of the stall Liffey was hiding in. It was uncanny. How could she have known it was Liffey in there?

Everybody on earth at that feis was wearing poodle socks and ghillies but Aunt Jean somehow found her with one knock. Now her aunt was back in tow and that meant Liffey would have to be back on therapist duty.

Before her aunt could launch into a non-stop narrative about her day, Liffey pretended not to have heard her and stepped up her pace towards the results board, oblivious to her aunt's chattering directly behind her. There it was. The number **777.**

It was in the **FIRST PLACE** box of Liffey's Novice **Hornpipe** competition!

"Didn't you place Liffey, darling?" Aunt Jean shouted sympathetically from somewhere in the crowd behind Liffey. "You and that silly Hornpipe have just got to make up and become friends. I know *just* how you feel, Liffey. Once I got a third place in my Jig and it was devastating." Liffey turned to her aunt and smiled absently.

Just as she was about to tell her Aunt Jean she actually had done very well in her Hornpipe, an announcement blasted over the hall intercom: "Attention. Your attention, please. Amanda Jackson, please come to the front desk immediately. Your parents are waiting for you."

Liffey froze. Amanda! That was the name of the little look-alike she had been worried about all day. She had apparently gone missing! Liffey knew now for certain that the feeling of dread and pins and needles she had been experiencing had been warning her that something bad was about to happen.

She should have paid more attention to her instinct and insisted that the little divas tell her more about Amanda so she could have gone to look for her. Now it might already be too late.

'That lady with the creature eyes. *She* has something to do with this. I know it! That's why I started following her. I should have never backed off when she humiliated me in the stairwell. I have *got* to find that woman!'

Liffey told her Aunt Jean, who had begun to describe her adult Slip Jig competition to Liffey in minute detail, that she would catch up with her later and before her aunt could protest, she darted towards the main lobby.

***

When Liffey reached the lobby, she saw a man and a woman who had to be Amanda's parents, standing at the reception desk, wild-eyed, staring at the desk phone. The woman was holding a baby boy who looked to be about eight months old. 'That would be her baby brother,' Liffey thought sadly.

There were three hotel employees behind the desk talking anxiously on their cell phones. 'They are keeping their desk phones free hoping that someone will call about Amanda.' Hotel employees began to congregate in the lobby.

Liffey realized she would have to make herself invisible so she would not be asked to leave the area because she was a kid. Liffey knew the drill. As soon as some adult noticed her, she would be ordered to leave immediately.

She found a luggage cart piled high with suitcases near the exit to the parking garage and crouched down behind it. Unless someone moved it, she would not be discovered and she could peek through the mountain of luggage to watch what was going on. Shrill sirens were approaching outside as the hotel security manager's voice addressed his staff: "You all know what to do. We have a missing child."

"A missing novice," Liffey thought, fighting back tears. We are all Irish dancers here and she is a **missing novice**."

The security man set up a large photograph of Amanda on an events placard in the center of the spacious lobby and handed out smaller photos of Amanda to the search group leaders. 'They have a missing child emergency plan in place,' Liffey thought, 'but that photo of Amanda they're using doesn't look much like her. It must be at least two years old.'

Police came pouring in through the lobby's revolving door and then blocked and sealed it with yellow tape. The hotel staff organized themselves into little search groups and set out to begin canvassing the hotel. Men in business suits wearing micro earphones appeared. They were each given the outdated photo of Amanda before they set off to do their own investigations.

Another voice blasted over the intercom: "Attention hotel guests. This is a missing child alert. The hotel is now on lockdown. No one will be permitted to enter or leave the premises until further notice. Please return to your rooms and turn your televisions to Channel 5 where you will see a photograph of nine-year-old Amanda Jackson. If you have any information as to the whereabouts of this child now or have seen her today, please contact the front desk immediately."

"Amanda was last seen in the hotel lobby waiting for her father who was checking out at the front desk. She is wearing a pink hoodie and jeans. She has a fever and may be disoriented. If you are not a hotel guest and visiting the hotel, please go to the Pittsburgh Steelers Ballroom and wait for further instructions. I repeat, this is a missing child alert. You may not leave the premises until further notice."

'Whew. This is becoming complicated,' Liffey thought. Taking advantage of the fact that she was a non-adult who would be pretty much invisible to everyone, Liffey decided to investigate the parking garage.

'Amanda was probably taken out that way.'

'So why is everybody just looking inside of the hotel? They should start with the parking garage.' The policeman guarding the garage door exit was a good fifteen feet in front of it. Liffey was between him and the door. She needed to move quickly if she were not going to be spotted by someone.

Liffey knew she would have to create a diversion of some kind before she could risk heading for the parking garage door. 'Otherwise, I will be caught.'

As if on cue, the mother standing by the front desk began to weep inconsolably. 'This is it. I am so out of here.' Liffey bounded towards the door behind the policeman while the entire lobby looked sympathetically at the grieving mother. The metal door opened easily and she was alone in the vast concrete parking garage.

"It is likely that if Amanda was waiting for her dad to check out, her mom had already gone ahead of the two of them and was putting the baby into his car seat," Liffey said to herself.

Liffey was right. Just a few feet away from the lobby door, she saw an unoccupied minivan with an empty baby carrier facing backwards, like before a baby weighs enough to sit facing toward the front of a car.

Somehow, Liffey knew that Amanda was not in the hotel now and that she had already been taken. She began to investigate the parking garage floor hoping no one would intercept her and drag her back into the hotel.

Nothing. There was nothing. Liffey could not see anything except a large oil stain on the concrete parking lot floor. She began to make her way back to the door and stopped a few inches away from the large oil stain. How had she missed this before?

On the grease spot, which she had carefully stepped around, about fifteen feet beyond the parked van, there was a peculiar pattern on the cement--several single right foot prints with smeared, dragging marks where there should have been a left foot imprint.

Step right, drag left. Step right, drag left. There were also little foot prints next to the large right footprint. 'Why was there only one large footprint? Nobody could walk on only one leg.'

The floodlights suddenly went on in Liffey's brain. *It was that old woman*, stepping down firmly with her good right foot and dragging her left leg along with her. The little foot prints belonged to Amanda.

Liffey shivered. She was right. The marble eyed lady *had* taken Amanda!

This somewhat relieved Liffey because she knew from her father's criminal law practice in Chicago that little old ladies, even creepy ones, are not normally child abductors. So then where was the old woman taking Amanda and why? After the large area grease spot ended, the trail disappeared with only a few smudges. Liffey took out her phone and took five pictures of the step and drag smear marks from different angles.

Just then the door to the parking garage flew open and Liffey could see three policemen walking quickly towards her. "What are you doing out here? Come with us and we will help you find your parents."

'Here we go again,' Liffey thought, as they grabbed her under her elbows and 'escorted' her out of the garage.

"Officers, I think I know who has Amanda!" Liffey blurted out.

"Oh you do? Well that's very interesting." They gave each other a maddening 'she's a cute kid trying to play detective' look.

"Yes! It's an old lady with blue marble eyes and orange, leathery skin. And she limps." This was a bit more detail than the police had expected.

"What makes you think that an old orange lady took Amanda?"

How could she tell them "Because I just know?" Liffey realized she needed to think a bit more about all this and do her own investigation. She needed more evidence.

"Come on little lady, let's get you back inside."

"Will you *please* just *look* at the footprints, officers?"

"Sure," a pleasant woman officer chimed in, obviously humoring Liffey. Liffey took them to the big grease spot and pointed out the step and drag marks and the little feet next to the large right foot prints. "All very interesting," one of the officers commented with no enthusiasm. "Now let's get you back inside the hotel and find your parents."

66

***

There was nothing more Liffey could do here in the garage with her 'escorts,' and she smiled and thanked the police officers when they turned her loose in the lobby. Liffey paused briefly as she brushed by Amanda's ashen faced parents and said: "Do you know that there is another Irish dancer who was at this feis today who looks exactly like your daughter, Amanda?"

Before they could reply or ask Liffey anything about what she had just said, one of the officers who had found Liffey in the garage approached them and angrily gestured at Liffey to get lost.

Liffey suspected there was some connection between Amanda's disappearance and the look-alike, but she could not think what it might be.

'Maybe the look-alike's mother was a psycho who had always wanted identical twins? I need to find out what dance school Amanda's twin goes to and then start asking questions,' Liffey thought.

She remembered one of the gigglers asking her why she kept asking Caitlin about Amanda. The little divas had been wearing their blue and white school dresses on their way to a figure dance stage this morning. Liffey wished now that she had paid more attention to the decorative symbols on their dresses because the colors blue and white belonged to several schools dancing here at this feis. Liffey walked quickly away from the lobby, determined to find a dancer who wore the same blue and white school dress as Caitlin and the other little divas.

Searching the hallways, it was not long before Liffey passed by an open suite door and saw three grief stricken dancers in familiar blue and white school dresses sitting on one of the big beds holding hands, while five adults stood together in the middle of the room, also holding hands, their heads bowed in prayer.

Liffey crept into their room, fairly certain that she recognized the school dress.

The circle of adults did not open their eyes. "Do you know where Caitlin is?" Liffey whispered to the three girls who looked about a year or so older than the giggling divas. "I think she's in U-10 Prizewinner," Liffey continued.

"Oh yeah! She's the one with the scary grandmother," one of the girls replied. Liffey felt pins and needles running up and down her spine. "Do you know where I can find Caitlin *and* her grandmother?" Liffey asked. "*Excuse me* but we are trying to pray for Amanda over here," one of the adults snipped from the prayer huddle.

'Well I might just be the answer to your prayers,' Liffey thought, trying hard not to say something sassy and rude that would anger these prayerful people.

"I'm sorry, it's just that I can't find Caitlin."

"Caitlin who?"

Liffey was frantically trying to think up a good last name for Caitlin when one of the girls on the bed saved the day and chimed in: "She's looking for Caitlin Cunningham, you know, the girl with that scary grandmother."

"Molly, please don't let me hear you talk that way. Caitlin's grandmother has cataracts. That's why her eyes are all cloudy. She can hardly see anything unless it is right in front of her face. And she drags her left foot because she had a stroke last year."

"They bring her along because Caitlin's family has three dancers and they want to have someone at each stage for moral support for each child. Even though she can't see very well, her grandchildren know she cares."

This information caused Liffey to pace back and forth like a panther in a small cage as she went over all the facts that Molly's mother had just provided. What had happened to Amanda was becoming crystal clear.

Liffey heard her own voice screaming across the room, like one of the little divas: "THAT'S IT! Amanda is *not* missing! Well, she *is* technically missing but she is fine!"

"I think that she is with the Cunningham family and the grandmother is the one who put her in their van. The granny can't see! She thought it was her granddaughter, Caitlin, sitting in the lobby chair. Since Amanda knew the old lady was Caitlin's grandmother and not a stranger, she took her hand and walked away from the hotel lobby with her to find her look-alike friend, Caitlin."

"When Amanda's father finished checking out, he turned around and Amanda was gone. The Cunninghams have not discovered yet that they have Amanda with them. Probably because Caitlin never said anything. Amanda got in the back of the van and fell asleep immediately because she is so sick. Caitlin thought that because her grandmother had opened the door for Amanda that she was supposed to be in there with them and the granny did not notice that her granddaughter, Caitlin, was already in the van."

"What makes you think that Amanda would not ask permission from her parents before going off with Caitlin?" Molly's mother asked.

"How did you figure all this out?" another adult voice questioned.

"Amanda was feverish and disoriented today," Liffey explained. "That's what the announcement said. I saw her playing last night at check-in with a group of young dancers from your school. They all seemed to be friends."

"Then this morning, she was nowhere to be seen and for some reason, I started to worry about her. These kind of weird worrying things happen to me all the time."

"Anyway, when I crashed into the grandmother several times today, she thought that I was not paying attention and she yelled at me like it was all my fault. Now I know how it happened. She could not see *me*! She crashed into ME! Then, she told me after I followed her that…"

"You *followed* her?"

"Why were you suspicious?"

"I don't know. I just was. So I checked the parking garage floor and saw that there were steps in a large oil stained area with a right foot and drag marks with a left foot. There were little footprints next to them."

"I knew then it was the creepy old lady—I'm sorry, I mean the nice grandmother with the bad eyes that had Amanda, because she limps. And since you told me she has cataracts, she obviously could not see the big grease spot and walk around it like a normal, seeing person would."

"I told the cops I thought an old lady with a limp took Amanda but they did not listen and told me to get lost. So I got lost right into your room and now let's get word to the

Cunninghams to check their van for twins and get Amanda back to her mother and father before they have nervous breakdowns."

The room was speechless.

A bossy-looking mother picked up the room phone and dialed the lobby while a man in the prayer group took out his phone and pressed a key. 'He's probably speed dialing the Cunninghams,' Liffey thought hopefully as she slipped quietly away into the hallway.

She did *not* want to be right in the middle of all the questions and attention that goes with solving a mystery. She *did* want some shrimp fried rice and some alone time to think about fate and her first place in her Hornpipe.

Was it only a strange coincidence that she got a first in her Hornpipe today? She would never know for sure. It was probably a combination of reading the last page of War and Peace as well as eating the spaghetti and meatballs pre-feis ritualistic dinner the night before.

Liffey waited in the hall for the elevator which would take her back to Aunt Jean and Max the Magnificent. She truly hoped Aunt Jean had done well today, because if she had done well, Liffey was going to suggest they go on a safari and then to a feis in South Africa. With Aunt Jean, anything could happen.

***

Driving on the Ohio Turnpike was like traveling through outer space. It was a place with no beginning and definitely no end. Aunt Jean switched on the radio for Liffey's Home

School daily history unit and said: "Today's current events are tomorrow's historical events, Liffey."

A reporter with a scoop from KDKA Radio Pittsburgh was interviewing an official spokesperson for the Pittsburgh Police Department.

"Thanks to some commendable detective work by our specially trained Missing Persons Unit, 9-year-old Amanda Jackson from Indianapolis, Indiana, has been reunited with her parents."

Another voice which sounded familiar said: "We were all praying." Aunt Jean turned off the radio.

"Liffey, I checked us out of the hotel from our room so we missed all the excitement in the lobby. Did you know that a little Irish dancer had gone missing?"

Liffey shrugged, smiled to herself and hugged Max the Magnificent closer.

Maybe it *was* the power of prayer that had led her into the praying room?

That, like her first place today in the dreaded Hornpipe, would probably remain one of life's unsolved mysteries.

THE END

THE CASE OF THE CLUMSY CLOWNS

"I have had quite enough of all this driving around on back country roads just to avoid passing by that harmless clown statue," Aunt Jean said in an irritated voice aimed at her niece, Liffey Rivers, who was sitting in the passenger seat next to her trying to become invisible.

Liffey nodded, but did not remove her hands which were covering her eyes.

"You are simply going to have to learn to face your fears, Liffey, darling, or they will ruin your life."

Liffey moaned. "Please Aunt Jean, I just can't today! I promise I will look at the clown statue the next time you drive by it."

"Soon we will be face to face with wild animals in the bush, Liffey. Eye to eye with beasts that would happily have us for dinner if we do not watch our step! One MUST learn to look at a clown if one is going to succeed on safari."

"How does 'one' succeed on safari?" Liffey mumbled to herself, somewhat annoyed with her aunt who always used the phrase 'one must' when she meant 'you must' if she was imparting what she considered to be important advice.

Liffey did not expect her Aunt Jean to understand why she was so frightened of clowns. She did not know the answer herself. She just was. Liffey had hated clowns as far back as she could remember.

She still had bad dreams about 'Mud Puddles,' the terrifying clown who had squirted streams of water at her little five-year-old-feet while she was standing on a sidewalk minding her own business watching the annual Clown Town parade with her father.

'I should have kicked him way harder,' Liffey thought, recalling how her father had to drag her away from the clown after she had delivered several painful kicks to the clown's kneecaps. "You are simply going to have to learn to face your

It had been quite a spectacle and Robert Rivers had taken her to a psychologist after this unpleasant incident to get counseling for her irrational fear of clowns which the doctor called 'Coulrophobia.' Eight years later, Liffey still did everything she could think of to avoid any kind of clown contact.

Aunt Jean was in high gear now. "The bush simply will not permit us to give in to our fears, Liffey," she said grimly, like some kind of wannabe safari guide. "We must master our fears before we depart on our great adventure. You MUST get over your Clownophobia!"

"I myself struggle with Toadophobia. I am terrified of toads, Liffey, if you did not already know this," Aunt Jean confided.

"Toads?" Liffey was very much surprised and tried not to giggle. She would have expected her aunt to be terrified of having a bad hair day or dark eyeliner running down her face. Not toads.

"Why would anyone be afraid of toads, Aunt Jean?"

"So why are **you** afraid of clowns, Liffey?" her aunt snapped right back.

They drove on in silence. Liffey did not want her aunt to work herself into a big hissy fit and quickly reactivated their conversation. "You are probably afraid of toads, Aunt Jean, because they are disgusting and people say they can give you warts. Who wouldn't be afraid of toads if you think about it? Daddy told me once that over near the Mississippi River in Mineral Point, the Cornish settlers used to put huge toads into big vats of fermenting apples that were

75

turning into hard apple cider. They thought that toad poop would make their cider taste better."

Aunt Jean shrieked and quickly pulled over to the side of the road, breathing in little gasps and holding her head melodramatically. Liffey immediately regretted telling her aunt the toads-pooping-in-the-vats story. She had obviously just given her aunt a whole new disgusting toad thing to think about.

"Oh well, pretty soon we leave for Africa," Liffey said cheerfully, realizing she needed to change the subject this minute as she opened the glove compartment. She handed her aunt the emergency brown paper bag they kept there for motion sickness emergencies. Aunt Jean placed the bag over her nose and mouth and breathed in and out while she was hyperventilating about toads.

"I know you will do *really* well at the feis in South Africa, Aunt Jean," Liffey continued. "Pittsburgh was just a warm up!" This was a brilliant thing to say because Aunt Jean was proud of her results at the feis in Pennsylvania and now thought she was destined for international glory and fame.

"Yes, I did do rather well, didn't I, Liffey dear?" she said, removing the bag from her face and smiling broadly.

"The life of an artist is full of ups and downs but mine is mostly full of ups because I eat right and point my toes at every given opportunity. For instance, look down right now at my foot on this brake pedal, Liffey. Can you see that I am flexing and pointing my right foot even while having this toad panic attack?"

Liffey began to compliment her Aunt Jean about the constant toe pointing but stopped mid-sentence and stared in horror at a huge sign in the church parking lot only a few feet away from the curb where they had stopped.

"Let's get going, Aunt Jean, or we might miss one of your soaps!" Liffey urged in quiet desperation, watching her aunt frantically rummaging through her purse looking for a peppermint candy to calm herself down. 'If Aunt Jean reads that sign, I'm doomed.'

Liffey sat perfectly still and held her breath, like there was a deadly, poisonous snake ready to strike a few feet away. She waited for the inevitable.

"Oh!" Aunt Jean exclaimed in astonishment popping the peppermint candy into her mouth and looking past Liffey at the large sign. It was over. Aunt Jean read the sign aloud with undisguised glee:

'COME AND WORSHIP JOYFULLY THIS SUNDAY AT 12:30 WITH THE CLOWNS FROM HEAVEN! BRING THE WHOLE FAMILY TO PRAY AND CELEBRATE LIFE WITH THESE JOYFUL JESTERS!'

"Liffey, darling, this is an answer to my prayer for your deliverance from fear of clowns!" Aunt Jean was overjoyed. "It is a direct message from heaven, Liffey! We shall attend this service together and you shall be healed and forever relieved from your irrational fear of clowns!"

"NO!" Liffey barked like a toddler having a tantrum. "NO! I am NOT going to celebrate life joyfully this Sunday with a bunch of stupid clowns!"

"Then HOW do you expect to **survive** in the bush, Liffey? Think about it. If you cannot even be in the same room with a few silly clowns, how do you think you will react when we meet one of the 'Big Five' face-to-face?"

"Now **which** animals are included in the 'Big Five,' Liffey?" Aunt Jean asked, rapidly down shifting into her home-school-of-life teacher quiz voice. Liffey answered her aunt mechanically in her pupil voice: "The Rhino, Lion, Leopard, Elephant and Cape Buffalo, Aunt Jean. These are the 'Must See Big Five' safari animals."

"That is correct, Liffey." Aunt Jean then returned to her regular voice. "So Liffey, darling, **how** do you think you will be able to manage when you find yourself eyeball to eyeball with one of the 'Big Five' if you cannot even sit in a church with joyful clowns sharing their joyfulness?"

"All right, Aunt Jean." Liffey knew when she was defeated. She would hear about these happy clowns all week if she did not just agree now to worship joyfully this Sunday with them.

"We will go check out the happy clowns on Sunday, Aunt Jean."

"**Joyful** clowns, Liffey. Being 'joyful' is more of a spiritual thing. We will be 'joyful' with the clowns and 'happy' when we meet up with the 'Big Five' animals on safari."

There was absolutely no doubt about it. Aunt Jean was completely nuts.

'Maybe I can be sick Sunday morning,' Liffey thought anxiously, her brain accelerating into survival mode. 'But Aunt Jean will see right through that.'

There *had* to be some way out of this! They could go out for a Sunday brunch at one of the snooty lake resorts. It was worth a try. If they arrived at 11:00 a.m., maybe she could distract her aunt and stall long enough by talking with one of the patient omelet chefs standing at attention behind their piles of ingredients, pretending that they cared deeply about brunchers like Aunt Jean and their important brunch choices.

'That could work. I could discuss each ingredient with Aunt Jean and the poor omelet chef and then ask her to teach me about how they all work together to help you to become a championship Irish dancer until we run out the clock. That will definitely work!' Liffey relaxed, confident now that she would be able to outwit Aunt Jean after all and avoid the joyful freaks.

Liffey was just about to start her plan and suggest that they go out to brunch next Sunday morning before they went to the joyful clown service, when she began to shiver and an icy feeling of dread crept over her even though she was not cold. There were little prickly pins and needles racing up and down her arms and back.

'Maybe the clowns really **are** going to try to get me!' Liffey thought frantically and began to search her memory bank again for a few backup excuses just in case her Sunday brunch idea was too lame even for Aunt Jean. But before she could think of a good backup plan, she felt her eyes being pulled up to the second floor sanctuary window of the old yellow brick church on the other side of the small parking lot.

There, through a thick, cloudy glass window pane, she saw a distorted white face with large blue lips and a bulbous blue nose staring off into the distance, its squinty little eyes looking above and beyond the parking lot like a ghost.

Liffey put her hands over her eyes again as Aunt Jean pulled away from the curb, rattling on about how they were going to eat Mexican food for lunch today and would Liffey prefer a taco or a burrito because they were both excellent sources of nutrition and they were only five blocks away from Hernandez's Restaurant.

Even though there was always the possibility that a clown piñata might be spotted hanging from the ceiling of Hernandez's Mexican Restaurant, Liffey was willing to take the chance that the place would be clown-free today. She was very hungry and had not had a good taco since the Pittsburgh Feis a few weeks ago.

She decided she would not tell Aunt Jean about the white faced clown with the big blue nose and fat blue lips that she had seen staring out of the church window. Aunt Jean would think that it was another 'sign' from heaven. The only reason Liffey had not completely become unglued and hysterical was because the monster clown had not been looking at her directly. It was gazing off into the distance. 'Probably plotting the end of the world,' Liffey thought grimly.

***

When Liffey Rivers had turned thirteen, she was told that it was time that she 'got a grip' and dealt with her irrational fear of clowns.

Before she became a teenager, if she spotted an evil clown at Hernandez's masquerading as a nice piñata, there was a procedure in place to handle the emergency. Liffey was to say 'clown,' and go immediately into the restroom.

While she was in there, the evil clown piñata would be discreetly taken down and purchased by Robert Rivers or her Aunt Jean. After it had been stuffed with delicious Mexican candies, it was sent across the street to the St. Andrew's food pantry.

Liffey knew her father and aunt had been very patient with her over the past clown infested years and expected her to cope now that she was older. However, seeing the hideous clown specter in the window just moments ago weakened Liffey's resolve to face her fears. She felt like runny jello.

'I need a poncho to hide under in case of a clown sighting,' Liffey decided, bracing herself as Aunt Jean bumped up over the curb trying to cram her pink Cadillac into a small parking space.

There were always lots of ponchos for sale in the waiting room right inside the entrance to the restaurant. 'If I tell Aunt Jean I'm freezing and that a poncho would make an interesting home school study unit as well as a unique adult Irish dance dress cover-up, she will definitely buy me one.'

"Aunt Jean?" Liffey asked, approaching the piles of colorful sombreros and ponchos and sarapes, "may I please have one of these ponchos? I am freezing to death and after lunch we could study it for a Mexican culture unit and it would make a unique and attention grabbing cover-up for you at feiseanna. You might even start a fashion trend. You know how you are always complaining that there are no sophisticated adult cover-ups."

Aunt Jean took the bait and immediately chimed in. "You are absolutely right about those tedious adult dancer cover-ups. I will certainly buy you a poncho so you do not catch a cold. Which colors do you think suit me best?"

"All of them would work, Aunt Jean. You can wear any color because you have a perfect complexion."

"How sweet of you to notice, Liffey, darling," Aunt Jean agreed. Liffey exhaled with relief.

"Seenyoor! Poor favwa, la blooah poonchow," Aunt Jean said, pointing to a sky blue poncho in a very peculiar accent. Aunt Jean's Spanish sounded like a tourist from China using a phonetic dictionary from Mars.

Mr. Hernandez pretended not to notice that her aunt was insane and handed the lovely blue poncho to Aunt Jean. He winced only a little when she said, "GraaaTH-ee-aTH, Seenoor!"

'Mexican Spanish does not use the 'th' sound,' Liffey thought, but her aunt never worried about the small details when she communicated with people. Like how to talk.

"I will definitely incorporate this poncho look into my signature Irish dancing fashion statement. This was a very good idea, Liffey, and I will make sure you get credit for it in my book. You may wear this lovely blue feis cover-up to warm you while we dine," said Aunt Jean, guiding Liffey's head through the top of the poncho.

"Thanks very, very much Aunt Jean!" Liffey said, sick of hearing about the future book, but very relieved that she could now take shelter under the poncho if need be. Aunt Jean smiled benevolently and went off to find the restroom.

Liffey pulled the heavy poncho up to eye level and began to move toward her favorite window table. If she saw a dangling clown piñata, she would pull the poncho up over her head before she passed by under it.

'I am **not** afraid of clowns. I am so NOT afraid of clowns,' Liffey told herself, determined to make it to the window table.

She had almost reached the middle of the dining room when it came into view. A huge blue Smurf dangling overhead. It reminded Liffey of the blue clown's nose pressed against the church window and before she could stop herself, she heard herself shouting, "Nooooo!" She pulled the blue poncho completely up over her head and stood totally still.

The headless poncho blocking the aisle in the middle of the restaurant caused a stir among the diners. The hum of lunchtime conversation suddenly stopped and all eyes were cast upon the motionless figure.

When Aunt Jean came out of the restroom, she picked up right where they had left off in their conversation about adult Irish dancer cover-ups. She did not even seem to notice that Liffey's head was not there and that there was nobody talking back to her.

"Yes, Liffey, darling, the more I think about it, the more excited I become! A poncho look is just what the drab world of adult dancer feis cover-ups needs. Now with the wigs, one must be careful when pulling the poncho over one's head, but other than that minor problem, it is a brilliant idea." Aunt Jean located Liffey's elbow and said:

"Come now, Liffey, let's walk over to our table and order some great big tostados with extra lettuce and naturally no sour cream full of all those ugly fats."

Aunt Jean guided Liffey over to a window table. Liffey allowed her eyes to peek out from under the poncho and was about to ask the dreaded question as to whether or not her aunt had spotted any clown piñatas when Aunt Jean, reading her mind, chimed in, "You don't have to remain undercover Liffey. I asked Seenooro Hernandez and he told me that he sold the last clown piñata yesterday. The ceiling is clown-free now, so you can come out and sit down and eat some of these wonderful taco chips."

Sometimes her crazy Aunt Jean was not so bad, Liffey decided, bobbing up to the surface from underneath the poncho like a turtle. Crazy aunts could be just what you needed if you were afraid of clowns. Nothing was too weird for Aunt Jean.

***

Driving by the Ronald McDonald clown guarding the McDonald's playground on the way home was the final leg of today's nightmare journey.

Liffey had always wondered why McDonald's had selected a clown to be its spokesperson to little children. If she had wanted a Happy Meal toy when she was little, she always insisted that her father use the drive-thru pickup window and covered her eyes until they were far away from the playground area where Ronald stood with his stupid smile.

Why adults deliberately inflicted clowns on innocent little children had always been a mystery to Liffey, but she had resigned herself to the fact that she would have to humor her aunt this Sunday and worship joyfully with the Joyful Jesters. Anyway, how could a bunch of stupid clowns performing in a church in the middle of nowhere be a threat to anyone?

"Aunt Jean, when we get home, let's skip the Mexican culture unit and practice our slip jigs."

"That is a marvelous idea, Liffey. We have no idea what our competition will be like in just a short while at the Johannesburg Feis in South Africa. I would think that they must be marvelous leapers, having learned to leap over poisonous snakes before they could even walk! We must make ourselves leap higher and hold ours a bit longer."

"You know, taking all the furniture out of the dining room and putting it into storage was a really good idea, Aunt Jean. It is nice having so much extra room to practice in. Daddy never thought of doing that."

"Well Liffey dear, your father is somewhat lacking in the imagination area. We both know how interested he is in boring history and all of those old things the ancients left behind them when they returned to their mother planets."

"Mother planets?" asked Liffey. This was a very bizarre statement even for Aunt Jean.

"Yes, Liffey. Mother planets are the planets the aliens came from before they landed on earth and erected things like the pyramids and Stonehenge. Your father loves to bore us all to death with historical theories about ancient civilizations when it has already been conclusively proven that all of the really old things on earth were built by people from outer space." Liffey nodded slowly.

"Why your father has to go on and on and on about how everything happened a long time ago is beyond me when it is all so simple. Just like in Irish dance, Liffey. It is beyond me why you yourself have to endure so many lessons and practices when it is all so very simple. Just point

85

your toes at every given opportunity and everything else will fall right into place."

"That's good advice, Aunt Jean," Liffey said slowly, wondering which mother planet her aunt had come from.

Aunt Jean had recently developed a habit when driving of pointing her right foot each time she switched it from the accelerator pedal to the brake. This caused the car to jerk a lot because her toe-pointing-foot often could not make it to the brake pedal fast enough to avoid hitting the car in front of her unless she braked hard.

Because of her erratic driving, she had been stopped several times by the local police who were suspicious of her lurching, and worse, Liffey had begun to get carsick almost every time she rode in the car with her aunt.

When Aunt Jean ripped around a corner like a movie stunt car driver, pointing her right foot twice in midair before she finally slowed down, Liffey wished that she had not eaten the third taco at Hernandez's and quickly reached for the brown paper bag in the glove compartment.

"Liffey darling, you must learn to control your nausea without the bag prop, just as you are learning to master your fear of clowns," Aunt Jean said perkily, completely oblivious to the fact that she alone was the cause of Liffey's recent problems with motion sickness.

Aunt Jean's toe pointing was getting so bad that Liffey had stopped going to her Irish dance classes. What was the point? She was so carsick when she got to class the last time that she spent the entire class period sitting on a folding chair watching dancers practice their double scissors and butterflies.

Just the thought of jumping up and switching her feet midair even once made Liffey feel even sicker, so she had reluctantly decided to take a break from Irish dance class until her aunt stopped driving like Mr. Toad.

Somehow, Liffey made it home without losing her lunch listening to Aunt Jean babbling on nonstop about "facing one's fears."

Liffey was tempted to tell her aunt about the huge toxic toads in Australia she had recently read about and the photo she saw of one of them that was fifteen inches long and weighed over two pounds. 'I wonder if Aunt Jean would be able to face her fear of toads and 'move on' if I told her about those toxic monster toads?'

At least those toads were far away in Australia. Clowns were right here in Wisconsin. Right here in Liffey's face. Maybe Aunt Jean was right about the mother planets. The blue nosed clown in the window Liffey had seen might very well have been sent by some unknown alien menace which was planning to rule the earth after it destroyed the human race.

Liffey shook herself. Aunt Jean was totally certified. There were no aliens long ago and certainly not right now. The creepy clowns who would be conducting this Sunday's church service were 'Joyful Jesters,' just stupid clowns, not other life forms from outer space.

***

Sunday morning came like it did every week. Right after Saturday night.

'If I can just make it to 12:30, it will be too late to attend the Joyful Jesters' service.' The radio alarm next to her aunt's bed and Aunt Jean's cell phone had been turned off.

Now it was only a matter of waiting and hoping her aunt would oversleep. As a final precaution, Liffey had tricked her aunt into staying up until 3:00 a.m. the night before discussing Irish dancing shoes. Aunt Jean was especially interested in the ones world champions wore and Liffey had managed to lure her online to see what all of her available options were.

If her aunt woke up before noon, the backup plan was to activate Lord of the Dance. It was highly likely that if Liffey could manage to start up a conversation with Aunt Jean about which female lead in Lord of the Dance would suit her aunt best, the good girl dancer or the bad girl dancer, she might be able to drag it out for hours. She knew Aunt Jean still thought of herself as a future star in an Irish dance show.

At 11:45 a.m., just when Liffey was beginning to feel like she had made it and thwarted the clowns' evil intentions, she heard Aunt Jean's voice ringing out from her bedroom like Big Ben. "Oh my! Liffey! Liffey, darling! Quick! I slept in! If we hurry, we can still get you to the church on time."

'Get **me** to the church on time? Like I am really going to go in there alone,' Liffey thought. Liffey knew that timing was everything in life so she pressed play and the first bad girl Lord of the Dance scene had just started when her aunt let Max outside. Liffey crossed her fingers when Aunt Jean walked hurriedly into the living room.

88

"Liffey, darling, we simply do not have enough time to study Lord of the Dance this morning. We must do the clown intervention first."

Liffey pretended not to hear her aunt. "Aunt Jean, do you think you would be the bad girl dancer or the good girl dancer in Lord of the Dance?"

"Hmm…. That is a *very* interesting question Liffey. It demonstrates that you are learning how to think and question the world around you." Aunt Jean had switched to her home school teacher voice which was a good sign. Liffey began to breathe easier.

"Of course I could easily do either role but I would never dye my beautiful natural blonde hair a darker color so I would have to refuse the bad girl dancer role and insist that I dance the good girl lead. Now hurry! Turn off the television. There will be plenty of time for us to discuss this interesting question after we attend the Joyful Jesters' church service."

Liffey moaned out loud. Not only had she failed to stop the clown confrontation, now she had doomed herself to spend the rest of the day after the stupid clown service talking endlessly to her aunt about which lead dance role suited her best. Like it was even her aunt's 'choice.' Like she could ever even get an audition. Like she was really a 'natural' blonde.

"Aunt Jean, may I please bring Max to the service for moral support?" Liffey pleaded.

"Certainly, Liffey, darling. We will smuggle him into the building inside my safari tote bag. It will be fine so long as he does not snore. He normally takes his first nap at noon so it should work. Where is his chewing sock?"

Very relieved that she would have Max with her for protection against a possible clown attack, Liffey reached under the coffee table and retrieved her terrier's sock of the week. When Max was a puppy, he could reduce a sock to threads in less than two days. Now that he was older, it usually took him five days to demolish one.

Even though it was only a seven minute drive to the yellow brick church, it seemed like hours to Liffey. Max the Magnificent weighed ten pounds but he was tough. If she gave him an attack command, she was confident he would move quickly to protect her.

Liffey had trained Max all week as a guard dog using an indestructible clown dog toy with an internal squeak mechanism she had ordered online the same day she had seen the blue nosed clown in the church window.

Liffey would toss it far across the room and yell: "Attack!" Max would bark fiercely and then tear across the room and sink his tiny teeth into the ugly little toy, making it squeak. Now Max was ready to be tested and Liffey knew he would measure up. If she could wake him up.

***

Liffey and her aunt made it past the toothy church greeter lady without a sound from Max. Liffey quickly scanned the almost full church. No sign of any clowns so far. Aunt Jean was understanding and permitted her to sit in the very last row of pews.

"If Max starts snoring or barking, I may need to leave quickly," Aunt Jean whispered. An organ started to play an unfamiliar hymn and everybody stood up and burst into song.

After what seemed like a billion long verses to a song Liffey did not know, everybody sat back down again and a loud drum roll sounded from the choir loft.

"A good morning to you ladies and gentlemen," an enthusiastic male voice announced like a circus ringmaster, "let's give a big Wisconsin welcome to the Joyful Jesters!"

Before Liffey could react, a mob of clowns wearing all kinds of terrifying makeup and costumes and wigs began making their way down the center and side aisles shaking hands with everyone and saying lame things like, "Don't worry! Be happy!"

Liffey put her hand deep down into the tote bag and felt Max's little jaw chewing on his sock. He was awake if she needed him.

When the sinister clown with the big blue nose and grotesque blue jester hat reached their pew and extended his blue-gloved hand, Liffey feared she might be his next victim. She put the tote bag on the floor sideways and tossed the clown toy she had hidden under her parka towards the blue nosed clown's feet.

Next, in a quiet but firm command voice, Liffey gave the order: "Attack!"

Max leapt out of the tote bag and ran after the indestructible clown toy but got confused and attached his little jaws around the real clown's ankle instead. The real clown screamed. "Get your vicious dog off me or I'll see you in court!" Max held on, growling and snarling, showing off for Liffey.

Aunt Jean slumped down in the shiny wooden pew and collapsed. Liffey was not quite sure what to do. Should she try to revive Aunt Drama Queen, who would probably then just go limp again, or risk approaching the blue nosed clown to pull Max off him?

Liffey knew the clown was faking the pain because Max's little jaws had very little clenching power. His tiny teeth were dull from years of chewing on socks. He never sharpened them on dog bones. Liffey decided she had better disengage Max from the wailing clown's ankle.

Two concerned ushers stretched Aunt Jean out flat in her pew with her head propped up and a million nosy people peered over their own pews trying to get a better look. Liffey did not want to think about how much trouble she would be in when Aunt Jean regained consciousness.

It had to be fairly obvious, even to her dippy aunt, that Max had been trained to attack the clown toy. Liffey forced herself to walk towards the clown. He was waving his hands above his head like an electric current was going through him and shouting like he was being eaten by a lion.

"Max! Stop!"

Max immediately let go of the clown's ankle and ran to Liffey. The clown stopped yelling and displayed a small hole located at the very bottom of the left leg of his blue clown suit.

'Max's little canines did not even leave a mark on this clown's ankle,' Liffey observed as she bent over to pick up her obedient terrier. It was clear that Max had only been tugging on the costume material, not chomping on the clown's ankle. 'This is just a pathetic sympathy ploy,' Liffey thought disgustedly. She knew little Max was not capable of hurting anyone.

Liffey mumbled an apology to the blue nosed clown and avoided making direct eye contact with its beady little eyes as she rushed past him towards the back exit door.

"Not so fast there, little lady." Liffey's skin began to crawl. "Where do you think you are going?"

'Is this thing talking to me?' Liffey halted. She could feel the entire congregation watching and listening.

"We are all here today to worship joyfully and that includes all creatures great and small. I am sure your little doggie did not mean to inflict pain and suffering and post traumatic stress on me."

Liffey quickly figured out that this Joyful Jester was talking lawsuit damages. 'Who does he think he's kidding? Max did nothing but tear his costume leg a little bit and I will compensate him for that.'

Liffey reached into her purse and took out her phone and the emergency fifty dollar bill she always carried with her. Then she asked the clown politely if she could take a photo of the tiny rip in his costume, waving the fifty dollars in his face. The clown snatched the money from Liffey's hand faster than Max the Magnificent had lunged at him.

Liffey quickly took a photo of the tiny rip as well as a close up of the clown's unbitten ankle and returned to the pew where Aunt Jean was now sitting upright. Ushers were fanning her face with church bulletins.

The greeter lady was holding Aunt Jean's limp left hand. Liffey noted the brave, glassy smile on her aunt's face. 'It is definitely time to go,' Liffey thought, when she heard loud sirens approaching the church parking lot. But before

Liffey could get her aunt's attention, the emergency exit door flew open and medical personnel raced into the church with a stretcher.

Aunt Jean looked like Cleopatra on a Nile River barge as they carried her out to the waiting ambulance. The congregation applauded like she was some kind of injured athlete. No one even noticed that Liffey was left behind all alone with the blue nosed clown and his creepy Joyful Jester friends.

"Where are the 'Big Five' when you need them?" Liffey grumbled, very much aware of the disapproving looks she was receiving from most of the worshippers. Even the children at this service looked at Liffey like they believed Max had actually hurt the evil clown.

'What kind of joyful clown snatches money from a kid's hand like that and threatens a lawsuit?' She sat down reluctantly and the service resumed. Her aunt would turn up sooner or later in a cab after she had soaked up all of the available attention at the local Emergency Room.

Max immediately fell asleep on her lap. "Good job, Max," Liffey murmured in his little, shaggy ear. The clowns began their performance. The red one was throwing a single crimson apple back and forth between his hands. "He's not juggling, he's playing catch with himself," Liffey told Max.

A clown with stringy yellow hair and a big red nose was jumping up and down in place. "Now that's hard." Another clown with a green face and white nose was standing perfectly still and frantically clapping his hands. The rest of the clowns were seated on the floor around these 'performers' watching their amazing feats. The organ began to play a haunted house kind of medley.

94

Liffey turned around and saw that the church organist had been replaced by a horrifying hobo clown wearing black and white makeup. The congregation seemed to be enjoying this stupid show. "These clumsy clowns obviously can't DO anything, Max. They are totally lame and this church audience is clueless. These clowns can't even juggle. Even I can juggle two apples."

The organ stopped abruptly. The Joyful Jesters linked arms, bowed, and then ran off the altar, waving like Irish dancers as they exited. People in the pews clapped enthusiastically.

'Am I losing my mind?' Liffey wondered. 'Exactly what did these so-called clowns actually do here today? Some entertainers.' Liffey was almost losing her fear of these clowns. They seemed harmless enough. Nonetheless, she felt very uncomfortable sitting here alone as the church congregation filed by her casting disapproving glances on their way downstairs for coffee and donuts.

Liffey was more or less stuck here in this church until her aunt returned. She yawned, thinking about the long, boring night she had spent with Aunt Jean yesterday online looking at Irish dancing shoes.

"You have the right idea, Max. I'm going to take a nap too." Liffey folded up her parka to use as a pillow and stretched out in the pew next to Max. The clowns would be downstairs with their fan club so she was safe for the time being.

It was the prickly pins and needles crawling on Liffey's skin that woke her up. She had no idea how long she had been asleep. Something instinctive told her not to sit up and reveal her presence when she heard deep, hushed voices coming from a just a few pews in front of her talking about when they should 'do the job.'

'Do what job?' Liffey was hardly breathing now. What if they saw her? Who were they? She dared not look and said her first prayer of the day: "Please do not let Max snore!"

"I'm telling you, if we go in now, it won't work. We need to bring in the quartet," a raspy voice argued.

"Are you joking? The quartet will take it themselves if we don't watch them 24/7."

"We came this far without them. Why should we bring them in now?" asked a high pitched voice.

"Because I have a bad feeling that someone is on to us." Liffey was certain that this voice belonged to the blue nosed clown.

"Yeah right," a nasal voice honked. Liffey could hear big feet shuffling away toward the altar. "Do you really think these Sunday morning lame brains are going to catch on?"

The blue nosed clown's voice answered: "It's not them, it's something else. I'm telling you, we need to bring in the quartet or this won't work."

The clown voices moved out of range just as Max suddenly exhaled loudly and began to sputter and snore. Liffey breathed a huge sigh of relief. She was sure she had been unintentionally eavesdropping on the clowns and it was obvious that they were up to something. She had distinctly heard one of the clowns call their congregation audience, "Sunday morning lame brains."

Whatever they were up to, Liffey was determined to stop them in their tracks. When Aunt Jean came for her, she would not tell her aunt that the Joyful Jesters were criminals plotting some kind of 'job' because Aunt Jean would never believe her. Especially after the Max incident. Liffey would have to apologize to her aunt and tell her she was finally ready to face her fear of clowns.

'The clowns are scheduled to be here at this church two more times. I will know they are ready to make their move when I see the quartet. But four of *what*?' Liffey googled 'quartet' and quietly left the church with Max.

It was almost 4:00 p.m. when Aunt Jean returned from the hospital in a shiny yellow Ford that said 'Mackie Taxi' on its doors. Liffey had been waiting for two hours in her aunt's pink Cadillac with Max on her lap, watching a young man across the street waxing an old white Mustang and thinking about quartets.

The clowns' conversation played over and over in her head: "I'm telling you, we need to bring in the quartet or this won't work."

'*What* won't work?' Liffey was clueless. When she had searched for the word 'quartet,' she found that 'quartet' could mean four of almost anything.

A barbershop quartet.

A string quartet.

A brass quartet.

A Gospel singer quartet.

Four of 'almost anything' was a lot to think about. 'It could even be a nickname,' Liffey thought.

Not to have heard more of the clowns' discussion was frustrating. 'They might have said something important that would make sense to me.'

The only other words Liffey had been able to make out as the clowns walked back towards the sanctuary and went completely out of earshot, sounded like gibberish: "Murf, surf, eagle." Then the voices were gone.

Liffey jumped out of the car and opened Aunt Jean's taxi door. She braced herself for a stern lecture and possibly way worse. 'I probably deserve to be punished this time because I completely overreacted when Mr. Blue Nose reached for my hand.'

Aunt Jean frowned a bit at Liffey like she was trying to decide what the punishment should be. Then she started: "Liffey, darling, I am sooo sorry it took me so long to get back here. The doctors said I was in shock and needed to lie still for a few hours before I was fit to drive."

"I should have called you, but while I was lying in the ER cubicle, I went into a deep meditative trance, and after careful deliberation, I came to the conclusion that I would actually prefer to dance the bad girl lead in Lord of the Dance because it would allow me to display my acting ability as well as my dancing technique."

"I am even willing to have my hair dyed black for art's sake." Liffey wanted to ask, "Art who?" but did not because she was relieved her aunt seemed to have already forgotten the crazy scene with Max the Magnificent in the church. It was impossible to ever predict what Aunt Jean would do because she changed her mind about things faster than a green chameleon turns brown on a twig.

"We must get back to work, Liffey," Aunt Jean said, jamming the key in the ignition and pointing her right foot before taking off. "Time is of the essence. South Africa is almost upon us and we cannot allow ourselves any more setbacks." Liffey wondered what the other setbacks had been but agreed wholeheartedly with her aunt that it was definitely time to seriously work on their Irish dance steps.

When they got home, Aunt Jean went into a kind of frenzy, blasting Irish dance music and leaping around the empty dining room. "We will practice eight hours a day from now until the feis in South Africa, Liffey. Nothing shall be permitted to interrupt our dancing. Nothing! We shall not stop for lunch. We will only allow ourselves to eat breakfast and dinner."

Once, Liffey had heard her father describe Aunt Jean's behavior as 'manic.' Watching her aunt flying around the dining room like this must have been what he was talking about.

Monday morning, driving into town for a blast off dance marathon breakfast, Liffey decided it was important for her to quickly figure out what the 'job' was that the clowns were going to do.

She had suspected they were up to no good the first time she had felt the warning shivers and spotted the blue nosed clown staring out of the church window.

"Aunt Jean, may we please drive by the church parking lot sign today to see what the Joyful Jesters are announcing for next Sunday?"

Aunt Jean smiled triumphantly. "Certainly. This is a major step in our clown intervention therapy, Liffey, and I am so very, very proud of you. We shall indeed go and look at the sign."

Even though Liffey Rivers was used to the earth going off its axis regularly in her young life, nothing could have prepared her for the jolt she felt when her eyes scanned the large, portable church parking lot sign:

'COME HEAR MATTHEW, MARK, LUKE AND JOHN, THE FOUR EVANGELISTS, THIS SUNDAY. THEN LET THE JOYFUL JESTERS LIFT YOUR HEARTS HEAVENWARD.'

***

"Hello! Anybody home? Liffey, dear, what will you be having for breakfast this morning?" asked Aunt Jean, interrupting Liffey's stupor. Liffey knew now that that the clowns must be getting ready for '*the job.*'

The sign announced that the 'four' evangelists were coming next Sunday. Were they the quartet? She had not been able to sleep the night before trying to figure out what the 'job' that needed the 'quartet' might be. Were they going to rob a bank? If so, why would they pose as clowns with a 'Joyful Jesters' ministry? Surely there must be an easier way to rob a bank?

"Hellooo! Liffey, darling, this lovely waitress has been patiently waiting for your food choices."

"I'm sorry! I will have orange juice, two eggs, two slices of bacon and an order of hash browns, please." Liffey was surprised that her aunt did not try to convince her to have a 'light' breakfast. She wondered if her aunt would order a predictable lettuce salad with a side of carrots and celery.

"I will have a tall stack of pancakes with two pats of real butter, maple syrup and three sausage links, please." Liffey was shocked. 'I guess Aunt Jean has finally come out of the cabbage patch.'

Her aunt began to browse through the Milwaukee Journal Sentinel morning newspaper and sip her coffee. Liffey remembered that she had not yet googled the words 'murf, surf, and eagle.' Even though she was fairly certain that she had not heard the words correctly when she was hiding in the pew, it was worth a try to see if she would get any hits online.

"NO WAY!" Liffey blurted out loudly.

"Liffey, darling, why are you yelling at your phone?" Liffey was too excited to answer. There was a *man* called 'Murph the Surf' who had pulled off the biggest jewel heist in American history in 1964 at the New York Museum of Natural History. One of the stolen jewels was the EAGLE DIAMOND!

"Liffey, aren't you going to eat your breakfast? You will need the calories for our dance marathon today and calories are much more important than nutrition."

Liffey forced herself to nibble on a slice of toast while she read on. Apparently, 'Murph the Surf' was still alive and had become a well respected minister after he was released from prison.

"So he is probably not one of the clowns here," Liffey whispered to herself. She ate another bite of toast when Aunt Jean peered over her newspaper and gave her a disapproving 'why are you not eating?' look.

Apparently all but two of the stolen jewels had been recovered. The extraordinary Star of India and 16.5 carat *Eagle Diamond* had never been found! Liffey tried to eat the rest of her breakfast to ward off more dirty looks from her aunt.

She felt flushed and shivery as she searched for 'Eagle Diamond.'

"Oh my! Liffey, turn around and look!" said Aunt Jean. There was a commotion at the café door and the breakfast eaters began to laugh and point at the five clowns bursting through the door with noisemakers.

These uninvited merry pranksters went all around the restaurant wishing everyone a joyful day and handing out lollipops.

Liffey did not see the blue nosed clown until it tapped her from behind on her left shoulder and snarled, "How's your little dog?"

Liffey broke into a cold sweat when she realized her phone screen with a full page photo of the Eagle Diamond was clearly visible to the clown. How long had **IT** been standing there behind her?

She forced herself to look past its ugly yellow teeth and bulbous blue nose directly into its eye slits and quickly snapped her BlackBerry shut.

A detached, far away voice answered the clown: "Max is just fine, thank you and looking forward to meeting the Four Evangelists next Sunday. What does one call four of something? A quartet I think?"

The blue nosed clown started to reply but could only manage a strangled gurgle. Liffey kept a plastic smile on her face until the clown slowly turned its back on her and quickly walked towards the other Joyful Jesters and gathered them into a huddle. Now she was certain that the clown had seen the full screen photo of the Eagle Diamond she was looking at when it snuck up behind her.

"Aunt Jean, I don't feel very well. May we please go home?" Liffey asked. She needed to get away from this town where clowns appeared out of nowhere like creepy crawlers. Go home to think. She had to figure out what to do now that she knew that Mr. Blue Nose knew that she knew the clowns were after the Eagle Diamond.

***

"The time has come for a makeover, Liffey," Aunt Jean announced perkily Monday night after dinner. Tuesday morning, she set off for an appointment with a hair color specialist. Liffey was glad to have some alone time while her aunt reinvented herself at the salon. It was hard to think clearly with Aunt Jean's constant chattering.

Liffey had to admit she was stumped. Even though she was certain that the clowns must know that the Eagle Diamond was either in the vicinity or soon going to be, she had very few facts to work with other than the history of the diamond itself.

The legendary Eagle Diamond had been discovered in Eagle, Wisconsin, in 1896 by a man digging a well in his backyard. There had been a frantic, mad rush to find more diamonds but not one single diamond was ever discovered after the fabulous 16.25 carat Eagle had been dug up.

Disillusioned and exhausted to the bone, hundreds of diamond hunters gave up their prospecting dreams and left town. Scientists said the lone diamond must have been moved to Wisconsin by a glacier during an Ice Age.

Liffey could not think of any logical reason why jewel thieves would dress up like clowns, put on totally pathetic shows inside a church and then parade around all over town with noisemakers handing out candy. It seemed ridiculous and way too complicated. And thieves were supposed to try to be invisible, not the center of attention.

'The center of attention!' Liffey flashed back to the Sligo Town train station where a few months ago she had struggled with a bad asthma attack.

At first she had been panicked because she knew her breathing difficulty might draw attention to herself from the police who had met the Dublin to Sligo train she was riding on looking for an American girl named Liffey Rivers.

Since there had been nowhere to hide, she boldly stepped directly in front of one of the policemen and used her inhaler, hoping that by placing herself center stage, she would become invisible. It had worked! The officer looked concerned and asked if she needed help. She smiled bravely and shook her head 'no.'

Then she strolled right past the entire police line holding her breath and clutching her inhaler. The clowns were doing the same thing! They were deliberately placing themselves front and center so that when they made their move, no one would notice anything unusual.

When the time came to execute their plot, everyone in town would be used to them running around acting stupid.

Just when Liffey's frustration level peaked, Aunt Jean returned from makeover land with her new coal black hair. She did not even ask Liffey about whether or not the new color suited her. Instead, she beckoned Liffey over to the living room coffee table and spread out the local newspaper.

"Liffey, darling, next Sunday afternoon there will be a train transporting antique circus wagons from Circus World Wisconsin stopping here. It will stay for one hour before it heads out for a Christmas circus exhibit at the Museum of Science and Industry in Chicago. Clown alleys from all over Wisconsin will meet and greet the train."

"Clown alleys?" asked Liffey.

"Yes, Liffey, clowns belong to alleys just like geese belong to gaggles and Irish dancers belong to ceilis."

Liffey knew her aunt had no idea what a clown alley was. Ever since she began homeschooling her, Aunt Jean seemed to have an immediate answer for any question Liffey asked. Liffey was sure she made many facts up.

"Do clowns really live in alleys, Aunt Jean?" Liffey pictured thousands of creepy clowns sleeping in abandoned warehouses in deserted alleys.

"They do not *live* in the alleys, Liffey. They *belong* to alleys. Apparently there is to be national media coverage with a helicopter following the train. Non-clown people are being asked to dress up like real clowns to greet the train! How exciting, Liffey! We will dress up like clowns and then worship with the Joyful Jesters."

"After church, there will be a clown parade heading down Main Street to the train tracks. Maybe we will be on television if our costumes stand out! What a glorious day it will be, Liffey!"

Aunt Jean looked victorious and radiant and went off chattering about colorful fabrics and rainbow clown wigs.

'Good,' thought Liffey. 'No more eight hour dance practices. Aunt Jean will be totally preoccupied with clown costume designs all week and leave me alone. I need time to figure out where the Eagle Diamond is and what in the world it has to do with clowns.'

If hundreds of clowns were going to meet the circus wagon train next Sunday, the Joyful Jesters would blend right in. 'They will be invisible among all those other clowns, but what does this have to do with a missing diamond?'

Liffey felt a familiar surge of adrenaline. It was obvious! The Eagle Diamond was going to be on one of the circus wagons headed for Chicago and the Joyful Jesters were going to try to intercept it! What better disguises could jewel thieves hope for? They would grab the diamond and then blend into a sea of clowns. They could then casually walk back to the church and change into street clothes.

A few things did not make sense. Why would the Eagle Diamond not be traveling in an armored car? And as far as Liffey could determine, the diamond had nothing to do with circuses before it was stolen from the New York museum. Why then would the Eagle Diamond be on a train carrying old circus wagons?

There was no news online about finding the lost Eagle Diamond. Just the old history facts. If Liffey's theory was correct, the diamond would be traveling secretly to another location in Chicago.

Liffey remembered seeing hundreds of precious stones in the Hall of Gems at the Chicago Field Museum on an eleventh birthday outing with her father. Could the lost Eagle Diamond be headed to the Hall of Gems?

The Museum of Science and Industry where the circus wagons were going was only a few miles away from the Chicago Field Museum.

'Time to play detective,' Liffey thought. She found the phone number and then dialed the Field Museum.

"Hello, may I please speak with the Hall of Gems?" Liffey panicked when she realized she had no idea what she was going to say if she actually reached someone.

"This is Kay Fitzsimons, may I help you?"

Liffey gulped. It was definitely time for her to say something intelligent.

"Yes. This is the Baraboo Wisconsin Security Office. I need to verify the ETA for the Eagle next Sunday."

"It should be approximately 4:00 p.m."

"Who did you say you are?"

No suitable reply to that question came into Liffey's brain so she rudely hung up. She had learned enough. The Eagle Diamond was en route to the Hall of Gems at the Field Museum which was only a stop before the circus train's final destination. Somehow, the Joyful Jesters knew this and were planning to intercept the jewel when the circus train stopped for the clown rally.

There had to be an insider accomplice who set this up. Liffey was certain Mr. Blue Nose did not have enough brain function to orchestrate such an elaborate plan. No one would expect a priceless jewel to be traveling on a circus wagon exhibit.

Liffey realized there was nothing much she could do during the week to prepare for next Sunday's drama. She would have to follow Mr. Blue Nose on Sunday and make sure she did not let him out of her sight. In the meantime,

'I can practice my slip jig this week without Aunt Jean flying all over the room like she is playing in a Harry Potter quitich match,' Liffey smiled.

She had heard Mr. Blue Nose say that the clowns needed the 'quartet' to successfully carry out their 'job.' Liffey shuddered. Her mind was racing. Who were *they*?

'They' would be at church dressed up like the Four Evangelists from the Bible: Matthew, Mark, Luke and John. So they were men. They could be dangerous. They might have guns.

'The diamond will probably be deposited in a safe under heavy guard on the circus train. Maybe the quartet were explosive experts?' Liffey knew this scenario was a bit Hollywood, but if she had learned anything in her almost fourteen years of life, it was that drama and chaos seemed to follow her wherever she went. Even to church.

✳✳✳

Liffey decided to leave Max at home and not bring him back to church for another clown confrontation. Aunt Jean had decided the two of them would be Irish dancer clowns with red curls and pastures of shamrocks painted all over their faces. Liffey knew they looked ridiculous in their bright Kelly green matching clown suits but Aunt Jean was clueless as usual and was thinking about starting up an Irish dancer clown alley.

When they arrived at church for what Liffey knew would be the grand finale of the Joyful Jesters, even though they were scheduled for next Sunday as well, she tried to remain calm. She asked Aunt Jean if they could sit up front in the first pew. It looked like the entire congregation had morphed into clowns.

The service began with Clown Blue Nose running down the center aisle loudly announcing that the Four Evangelists had arrived with good news from the Gospels. Then there was a trumpet blast from the choir loft and the four hooded Evangelists walked out from the sacristy on to the altar and turned their backs to the crowd.

Liffey tensed. A dreadful thought occurred to her. 'What if the Four Evangelists were going to hold them all as hostages in exchange for the diamond when the train arrived?'

The first Evangelist turned around and faced the congregation. Liffey's heart was pounding. Then she heard a disembodied voice shout: "WHAT IS THIS?"

Aunt Jean was aghast and shushed her: "Liffey, darling, remember you are in church!"

The first Evangelist was Mrs. Pamela Frost, Liffey's third grade Reading teacher. Mrs. Pamela Frost did not seem to recognize the petite green clown who had so rudely shouted out from the first pew.

The other three evangelists were women too. The skinny lady who ran the local bowling alley, the hair colorist who had colored Aunt Jean's hair coal black so she could be the bad girl dancer in Lord of the Dance, and a waitress from Hernandez's Mexican Restaurant.

Mr. Blue Nose stood on a low stool, head bowed reverently in pretend prayer with his three floppy jester hat tails drooping.

'This is *not* the quartet!' Liffey had been *completely* wrong suspecting that the Four Evangelists were going to be the blue nosed clown's accomplices. But if *they* were not the quartet, then who?

Time was running out. The circus wagon train was due in forty-five minutes. Just forty-five minutes to stop the lost Eagle Diamond from going missing again, maybe this time forever.

The Joyful Jesters seemed to be in high lunatic form, jumping up and down in place on the altar and flapping their arms around like grounded birds. Liffey studied Mr. Blue Nose carefully. He was not 'cool.' She had seen him crack at the restaurant when she asked him what 'four of something' was called and little beads of sweat had started to run down his greasy white face paint.

Liffey had learned from her father that guilty people often display body language clues. 'If I can agitate Mr. Blue Nose again, maybe he will look at the quartet if they are in here in this church.'

Liffey decided to take drastic action. She jumped out into the center aisle and launched into her soft shoe jig, keeping her eyes fixed on Mr. Blue Nose. She hoped he would quickly focus his eyes on something specific and was not disappointed. He glanced nervously far back into the congregation on the right side.

'The quartet is back there!' Liffey spun around and did one-two-three's down the aisle and around to the right where she saw four identical Hobo clowns sitting together in the back pew with their sad faces and baggy suits and derby hats. They had painted on beards and big red noses. 'This *had* to be the quartet!' Blue Nose had directed her to them with his GPS tracking eyes!

Liffey switched to her Slip Jig and traveled back up to the altar where she bowed to the startled Evangelists and clowns like they were feiseanna judges and slid back into the pew next to Aunt Jean who was beaming with pride.

The congregation was shocked and stared coldly at Liffey and her aunt who was applauding enthusiastically.

"What an amazing, stunning finale to your struggle with Clownophobia, Liffey, darling! Joyfully jigging and then bowing humbly to the Joyful Jesters! I am utterly speechless and so very proud of you!"

Liffey smiled weakly. Thirty-five minutes. Her head began to throb when she realized there was no longer enough time to put together all of the missing puzzle pieces.

Then, from out of nowhere, like the sun coming out from behind dark rain clouds, the realization dawned on her that she had been completely WRONG about the Eagle Diamond being on the circus train!

The Eagle Diamond was already here! Liffey had clearly heard the blue nosed clown say, "If we go in now, it will never work." Like he was being pressured by the other clowns to get the diamond, wherever it was, *before* the circus train came, after which they would need the quartet to help them.

Maybe these clowns were not quite as stupid as they looked. They obviously had a well-connected informant somewhere who had clued them into the whereabouts of the diamond.

When Liffey had called the museum in Chicago, the woman she talked with confirmed that the 'eagle' was expected around 4:00 p.m. on Sunday.

111

The clowns obviously knew this too and they also knew where the diamond was being kept *before* it was going to be transferred to the museum. Since Mr. Blue Nose had said he had "a bad feeling this time," they waited for the quartet. Try as hard as she could, Liffey could not figure out why the mysterious Eagle Diamond would be here in her little town in the middle of nowhere. Liffey could not think of any possible connection between the diamond and a circus train stopover.

Aunt Jean's loud whisper pierced Liffey's clogged brain when the offering basket began to be passed on the other side of the aisle by *another* clown dressed like a Hobo who looked almost exactly like one of the quartet.

"Liffey, that's 'Tramp.' I met him last Wednesday at my new clown alley meeting. His name is James Bowman. They say he is an eccentric, kind millionaire do-gooder. Clown Sonny Boy told me Mr. Bowman joined our clown alley in honor of his great-grandfather who was a famous Tramp clown from Eagle, Wisconsin."

"In fact, he also told me the reason the circus train is stopping here on its way to Chicago is because Tramp paid a lot of money to ride on it incognito. Isn't it exciting? I think one calls it riding the rails."

Bingo! The lights went on in Liffey's head and her skin was tingling. Tramp had the diamond on him right here. Right now! Possibly hidden under his big red nose. After church, he planned to walk to the train and discretely board it as it pulled away. A bit strange, but according to Aunt Jean, rich, philanthropic people were often oddballs.

112

He was then going to deliver the Eagle Diamond to the Field Natural History Museum around 4:00 p.m. to honor his great-grandfather.

'That must be why there is going to be a helicopter following the circus train.' In Chicago there would be a news conference at the museum and the diamond would become part of a permanent display. Just like it had been in New York until it was stolen.

Liffey wondered how he had located the Eagle Diamond and how much he had paid for it. 'He must have spent a fortune buying it and then paying off the insurance company who had already paid the museum in New York for the loss of the famous diamond.'

Twenty-five more minutes. It was obvious to Liffey that the quartet and the Joyful Jesters were going to assault Mr. Bowman, steal the diamond and then get out of town fast. If anyone witnessed the crime, there were already at least five Hobo clowns in this church alone.

'They must be planning to steal the diamond during the clown parade. If they pulled off Tramp's nose, which would be the safest place to transport the gem, the robbery would look like a funny clown skit. No one would know that what they were witnessing was real.'

Liffey had to warn Tramp that he was in extreme danger, but since adults rarely paid attention to anything she said, and there was very little time remaining before they would leave to join the parade in the center of town, she had to move fast. Somehow she would have to keep the quartet and clowns here in this church so Tramp could make it to the circus train safely.

When Tramp and the money basket reached Aunt Jean, Liffey again jumped out into the aisle and hugged the Tramp clown.

The congregation was not amused and this time shouted advice like: "Get back in your seat!"

Liffey quietly whispered in the clown's ear, "Mr. Bowman. The other Hobos in this church know you have the diamond and they are planning to rob you."

"As soon as I stop hugging you, you must act disgusted, point to my pew and order me to sit down. Then take the collection basket to the back of the altar and slip out the back door. Leave immediately. I will create a diversion and keep everybody in here. Go quickly!"

For once, an adult took her seriously. The Tramp clown shook his head disgustedly, pointed to her pew, and loudly ordered her to, "Sit back down immediately, young lady!" Then he walked to the back of the altar with the collection basket.

Aunt Jean was fanning herself and beginning to look like she might faint again. Mr. Blue Nose turned rigid and looked back at the quartet again.

'You idiot,' thought Liffey. 'You should be looking at Tramp!' Liffey knew she would have to go pretty far out on a limb to get this church secured before the clowns figured out that Tramp had slipped out the back door.

There was only one thing she could think of that would cause an immediate lockdown: A homicide!

She dialed Emergency 911 on her cheap phone with its pre-paid-for-minutes which she used when she wanted her calls to be untraceable. She quietly reported a murder might have taken place at the church.

Liffey was fairly certain that this would lead to her *own* homicide if her aunt figured out she made this call, but she could not think of any other way to save Mr. Bowman and the diamond.

Within seconds after her call, since the church was only a half block away from the police station and there were extra police on duty for the parade, the church was completely surrounded by police and sheriff's deputies with megaphones who were shouting instructions for everyone to remain in their seats.

Liffey sighed. Blue Nose blew it! The clowns should have 'gone in' to what was probably Mr. Bowman's home safe to get the diamond and not have waited to bring in the quartet.

Liffey settled back. It looked like she and her aunt were not going to see the circus train after all.

The Joyful Jesters showed their true colors when they figured out that Tramp had escaped out the back door. Every obscenity Liffey had ever heard came out of their clown mouths while the police, who were keeping everyone inside the church, interviewed people pew by pew.

'Those idiots are going to be arrested for disorderly conduct,' thought Liffey.

The Four Evangelists sat stone still on the altar and enjoyed the show. In back of the church on the right, the quartet pulled their derby hats over their eyes and appeared to be napping.

✳✳✳

On the television news that evening, Liffey watched a feature story about the Wisconsin Eagle Diamond which had been missing since 1964 and was now about to become a permanent exhibit at the Field Natural History Museum in Chicago.

The on location reporter narrated a video showing the Eagle Diamond donor, a Tramp clown, arriving at the Field Museum on a circus train and ceremoniously handing over a small box to a few museum officials.

After a brief presentation, the Tramp clown tipped his derby hat and re-boarded the circus train headed to its final destination at the Museum of Science and Industry.

Finally, the television cameras captured the Tramp clown climbing out of the train's caboose and leaving in a bright red helicopter. Liffey clicked off the television and gave Max a bite of her Hernandez bean burrito with extra guacamole.

THE END

THE MYSTERY OF THE TEMPORARY TROPHY

A unt Jean was suffering from Post Traumatic Bling Syndrome.

The doctor on emergency duty at the Liberty Torch Feis in New York told Liffey that he had been seeing more and more of this baffling disorder lately. Possibly because there were so many feiseanna these days.

Many Irish dancers were competing several times a month and some of these dancers would inevitably become

117

overwhelmed by all the glitter and sparkle and would not be able to cope.

While Liffey's peculiar Aunt Jean only competed at feiseanna occasionally, after Liffey told the doctor that her aunt had begun to talk endlessly about rhinestone poodle socks and colorful solo dresses decorated with hundreds of Swarovski crystals, the doctor said he was fairly certain that at some point Aunt Jean's brain had become dazzled.

Even though she had colored her dyed blonde hair coal black for the role of the bad girl in Lord of the Dance, Aunt Jean had apparently forgotten all about auditioning for the show and was now determined to become a famous Irish dance dress designer instead.

Ever since she had joined the local clown alley in Wisconsin and had become 'Clown Tootles,' Aunt Jean had been completely out of control. Liffey tried to be patient but it was difficult listening to her aunt going on and on about things like designing disposable paper solo dresses that could be thrown away after you danced at a feis.

Aunt Jean had a 'vision' of her solo dress designs morphing into short-skirted clown costumes covered with geometric shapes like triangles and squares and circles and diamonds. "My solo dresses will include color-coordinated clown noses which will match the dancer's dress. And there will only be rainbow colored clown wigs, Liffey. Enough of those long, boring curls. Enough of them! One can never have too much color, Liffey. Never!"

Liffey was seriously thinking about calling her father and unloading all of her concerns about Aunt Jean but decided to spare him for the time being. He already had enough on his plate. Liffey knew she should never have let Aunt Jean

118

talk her into going to a feis three days before they were leaving for South Africa. It had been way too much for her aunt to think about.

This New York Liberty Torch Feis was huge. There were at least 1,700 dancers. Many of them were leaping around in dresses smothered with twinkling bling. Liffey thought they looked like comets flashing through the sky when they danced.

It had all been too much for Aunt Jean to handle and she collapsed on stage right after she placed fourth in her Reel. When the EMT stretcher had deposited her aunt at the feis doctor's emergency station, Aunt Jean rallied and started talking about her design visions again.

The doctor listened carefully and diagnosed Aunt Jean's anxiety disorder. He patiently explained that with early intervention, the psychological trauma Aunt Jean had experienced as a result of being surrounded by so many sparkling stressors could be brought under control.

The doctor told Liffey to take her Aunt Jean back to their hotel room for absolute bed rest and not allow her to watch shows like *Dancing With the Stars* because that might worsen her condition.

Liffey agreed and thanked the doctor. She gently took Aunt Jean's hand and led her out of the medical station. On the way back to their room, Aunt Jean explained to Liffey that everything that really mattered in life was about sparkle and glitter and the evolution of clowns into dancers and vice versa.

"It will be a totally new art form, Liffey. Think of it. Feiseanna will be held under a Big Top tent. Adjudicators

119

will become a thing of the past. There will be three rings and a leprechaun Ringmaster."

"Instead of all those incompetent judges, there will be sophisticated applause meters and the audience will decide how a dancer places. That obsolete numbers scoring system used by the judges is not accurate. If it were, I would place first all of the time."

"At the end of each competition, dancers will step out of line individually and the applause meter will record the crowd's response. The dancer who receives the loudest applause will be in first place and so on."

"It's about time Irish dancing competitions became fair playing ground, Liffey. I certainly did not deserve the fourth place I received today. I will right this wrong by completely revolutionizing the Irish dance world."

After Liffey was sure her aunt was asleep under a fresh avocado face mask, she quietly crept out of the room and made her way back down to the feis. Aunt Jean had been too busy having her nervous breakdown to remember that Liffey was supposed to dance today too. However, Liffey was not so sure now that she wanted to go ahead with it. 'Aunt Jean is exhausting. I think I will just walk around for awhile before I make up my mind whether or not I am going to dance.'

Liffey entered an enormous results room where a special awards stage had been set up for the championship dancers. There were so many trophies lined up on the long platform that it reminded Liffey of a merchandise clearance sale.

She imagined herself standing center stage, high up on the first place winner's block. She was holding a large, shimmering blue and gold trophy. Her best friend, Sinead, was standing on the second place block and one of the evil, dark haired twins was standing on the third place block. Since they were identical, Liffey did not know which one of the twins it was. Liffey was delighted that she and Sinead had taken the first and second places. It was always nice beating the twins.

When the lovely daydream had ended, Liffey's eyes drifted over to the super sized perpetual trophies. 'If I won one of those, I would *never* return it to the feis committee to give to someone else the next year. They would have to track me down to find it. I would bury it in Max's dog bone graveyard or in the front yard under the oak tree. What is the point of a *temporary* trophy?'

While Liffey was contemplating where she would hide herself while the feis committee searched futilely for her and the perpetual trophy she had received the year before, she noticed that several temporary trophies on the stage were particularly impressive. She walked up the stairs to get a closer look at them.

One of them reminded her of the ornate chalices she had seen last summer with her father at the National Museum in Dublin. Most of those chalices had been buried in the Irish bog for centuries and discovered accidentally hundreds of years later.

Maybe Liffey would forget where she had buried her perpetual trophy and someone would accidentally dig it up when the land around her house was being bulldozed in 2300 for a new housing development.

'At the rate I am going, I would have to live to be at least 200 years old if I am ever going to be anywhere close

121

to being eligible to compete for a perpetual trophy,' Liffey sighed. She moved closer to the unusual trophy that had caught her eye. 'This one has a circle of embedded amber stones around the top of it.'

The other perpetual trophies were less impressive and appeared to be made from cheaper metals. 'The one with all the amber stones certainly looks like real gold and silver,' thought Liffey.

"Isn't it amazing?" a silky but somewhat bitter woman's voice asked from directly behind Liffey. "That one there you are looking at looks like it's made from real silver and gold doesn't it?"

Liffey felt pin pricking tingles running up and down her back and without turning around replied, "Yes, it does look real."

Liffey knew she was doing nothing wrong standing on the awards stage staring at this exquisite trophy, so why was she feeling shivery and disoriented, like there was a bright spotlight shining on her in a pitch black room?

She hesitated to turn around and make eye contact with the woman behind her who had just commented that the trophy looked like it was made from real silver and gold. The female voice had a nasty, accusatory edge to it. It reminded Liffey of her middle school Principal Godzilla's tone the day he boarded the school bus headed for a Six Flags Great America amusement park outing and removed her from the group trip of 'well behaved students' because he discovered that she had received a detention for being tardy that week.

What kind of word was 'tardy' anyway? Students are 'late' for school. Tardy was a word that belonged back in the Middle Ages.

Liffey got up the nerve to spin around. Whoever it was that had been standing at the bottom of the steps talking to her about the unusual trophy had vanished but Liffey was certain there was someone close by who was staring at her. She could feel the unfriendly eyes following her as she left the stage.

Liffey turned back around slowly to give the trophy one last scan before she left the results room. She was almost certain that she had seen this chalice cup someplace else before. It was mounted now on a large, square wooden box with little brass strips on all four sides which would be engraved one by one with the name of a new champion each year.

The front plaque on the bottom of the trophy box read: **'Liberty Feis: Murphy Family Perpetual Trophy.'**

Since there were no names engraved on any of the brass strips yet, Liffey knew this had to be the first year that this trophy was going to be presented.

There was only one place Liffey had traveled where she might have seen anything like this impressive Murphy Family Perpetual Trophy. It would have been in Dublin at the National Museum.

Liffey and her father had not been able to spend much time in Dublin last summer. They had to cram a lot of sightseeing into one afternoon. After they had picked up her first solo dress in Glasnevin, Liffey made up her mind to show her appreciation to her father by not acting bored when he dragged her all over Dublin telling her about Irish patriots.

The early part of the day had gone well. They had walked across the famous Ha' Penny Bridge arched over her namesake, the 'River Liffey.' She found the bullet holes in the Daniel O'Connell statue. She admired the statues in the General Post Office where the 1916 Rising had begun. They had tea while they watched street performers on Grafton Street.

They had even managed to go through the National Museum where they saw the real Tara Brooch and artifacts like the famous Ardagh Chalice and more ancient Celtic gold jewelry than King Midas could have ever hoarded in his palace.

It was in the late afternoon when Liffey noticed that her father had begun to act peculiarly while they were looking at the Molly Malone statue near Trinity College. He took her picture leaning against Molly's wheelbarrow and right after the photo, started hauling Liffey in and out of buildings and bus terminals and riding around in taxicabs all over Dublin like they were running away from someone.

He had told Liffey that they were jumping in and out of cabs because he wanted to compare the taxis in Dublin with the ones in London.

'I need to get some up close photos of this beautiful Murphy Family Trophy,' Liffey decided, coming back into the present moment. 'Then I can go find some food and do my chalice homework. I think I have seen it before.'

After rapidly ascending the stage again and taking six pictures of the trophy from different angles, Liffey walked quickly down the platform stairs through little clumps of dancers and their mothers who were sitting and standing around the stage area. She had probably imagined the warning shivers. No one seemed to be looking at her now as she began to make her way over to the U-13 Novice and Open stages. On January first, after the feis in South Africa, she would be in U-14.

The smell of nachos in the air directed her to make a sharp left hand turn out into the wide hotel hallway. She would get them with extra cheese and then begin an online google search of the National Museum looking for Ireland's medieval chalice collections and see if her suspicion was correct.

Maybe the Murphy family deliberately copied one of the chalices in the museum. That was probably legal. Could an ancient artifact in a museum be copyrighted?

Liffey knew she should be concentrating on this Liberty Torch Feis and make up her mind whether or not she was going to do any of her steps today. She had probably already missed both of her soft shoe competitions while she had been talking to the feis doctor. After the stressful ordeal with her aunt, she did not think she had enough of her own brain function left to do her Treble Jig and Hornpipe steps.

Since Aunt Jean was apparently sleeping off her nervous breakdown upstairs and all Liffey could think about at the moment was the intriguing chalice trophy, the decision not to dance today was final. 'If I don't do my steps today, I won't have to mislead Aunt Jean and tell her anything because Aunt Jean will be totally drowning in self-pity about placing fourth this morning because it was the last place in her adult competition. She will not even think to ask me how I did today.'

Liffey was sure that it would probably take many days of reassuring her aunt that she really was a great dancer and that the adjudicators here in New York were disgraceful before Aunt Jean would come around again.

'Aunt Jean has to be the most demanding person on earth,' Liffey thought. She found a secluded spot on the side of a temporarily-abandoned-for-lunch U-12 stage and sat down with her nachos and BlackBerry.

Even though she feared another confrontation with the scary woman who belonged to the sly voice, she was determined to investigate further. If she was not going to dance at all today, she had nothing better to do than play detective.

Liffey was happy to discover that Ireland's National Museum's website was easy to navigate. She immediately located the Irish antiquities collections and the beautiful Ardagh Chalice. It was similar to the perpetual Murphy trophy in style but nowhere near identical. It was much more elaborate.

Next, she found something called the 'Derrynaflan Hoard.' She looked around anxiously, saw nothing that alarmed her, and continued reading. It was made up of religious objects from the 9th century which had been hastily buried to hide them from the invading Vikings who were in Ireland raiding and looting everywhere they went. The Derrynaflan Hoard remained undiscovered until some people using a metal detector found it in County Tipperary in 1980.

After reading the history, Liffey scrolled down to the photographs of the early medieval Derrynaflan objects and smiled triumphantly.

"Yes! This is it! It's the Derrynaflan Chalice!" Liffey blurted out excitedly to herself when she compared her photo of the Liberty Torch Feis Trophy to the ancient jewel studded chalice. 'They are identical!' Information underneath the photo said in small print that the chalice had 54 embedded amber stones.

'The Murphy family seems to have made an exact replica of the Derrynaflan Chalice for their Liberty Feis perpetual trophy. I wonder why?'

Suddenly, Liffey felt little pinpricks at the bottom of her neck like the static electricity shock you get from the dry winter air when you touch someone or comb your hair with a soft bristle brush. 'I need to get back to that awards stage yesterday and count the amber stones.'

Liffey's mind was racing as she dialed her friend Sinead in Sligo.

"Liffey! Are you on safari yet? I am desperate to hear all about it!"

"No, Sinead. Not yet. I need you to do me a big favor. Could you please ask one of your brothers in Dublin to run over ASAP to the National Museum and count the number of amber stones on the Derrynaflan Chalice in the Antiquities section?"

"The *what, where?*" Sinead answered.

"The Derrynaflan Chalice in the National Museum. I think it's by the Ardagh Chalice."

"Oh sure, I know the Ardagh one," Sinead replied.

"My brother's place is close to Merrion Square. I'll ring him up and see if he can get over there right away. He doesn't work on weekends unless an illegal drug shipment turns up in a container. You're not getting yourself involved with something dangerous again are you, Liffey?"

"No. Really, I'm not! I'm at a feis in Libertyville, New York, killing time and I think one of the trophies here is a copy of the Derrynaflan Chalice. I just want to confirm it. I need to count the stones on the one here and then compare my count with your brother's count in Dublin. It's like the pearl counting on the Queen Elizabeth portrait in London, remember?"

"You can't be *serious,* Liffey? Just in case you have forgotten, that was a terrifying ordeal! You do *not* want to do that again!" Sinead protested.

"I totally promise you that I am not getting into anything dangerous. I promise. I just need to know how many amber stones there are on the Derrynaflan Chalice in the National Museum. When I find out, I will let you know what we need to do next.

"*We?*"

"Yes, *we,*" Liffey answered matter-of-factly.

***

Liffey realized it was not going to be easy getting back up on stage and casually standing around counting all the amber stones on the Murphy Family Perpetual Trophy. Some of the amber studs were in places which would require her to manually rotate the trophy for an accurate count and this would certainly draw attention to herself. She needed to get pictures from every angle so she could do a recount in private, without interruption.

The Murphy Family Perpetual Trophy competition, according to the Liberty Torch Feis syllabus, would take place this afternoon at 1:00 p.m.

It was not quite noon when Liffey walked back to the awards stage where dancers were beginning to gather waiting for their Prelim results. The stern looking stage monitor was patrolling the area like a guard dog.

Liffey could not shake the feeling that she was missing something obvious about this Murphy Family trophy-- something that had jumped out at her when she had first seen it but her brain had failed to process.

If she was going to get back up on the awards stage to count the stones, she would have to come up with some logical reason why she was so interested in this Murphy trophy. She needed at least ten uninterrupted minutes of staring and counting stones and taking more pictures. The stage monitor would probably tell her that the awards platform was 'off limits' unless she could think of a logical reason to be up there.

'I need to get back upstairs to check on Aunt Jean anyway so I will change into street clothes and say that I am a high school reporter doing a feature story for my school newspaper about the Murphy family Irish dancers at my school. That should give me the credentials to inspect the stage and take pictures.'

While she waited for the elevator, Liffey found an online list of Libertyville area high schools. 'If that stage monitor lives around here, she probably knows the names of all the district schools.' There were twelve Libertyville community schools. Ben Franklin High School was third on the list. 'Sounds good,' Liffey thought.

Unless she was going to have extremely bad luck and the stage monitor would know whether there were or were not Murphy family Irish dancers at Ben Franklin High School, it should work. 'With my track record, the stage monitor is probably the Ben Franklin vice principal, but at this moment, I can't think of anything else that will give me access to the awards stage.'

Liffey waited ten minutes for the elevator to arrive in the crowded lobby. When she finally reached room 610, she was dismayed to hear loud, thumping music coming through the almost sound proof door. 'What is Aunt Jean doing? She's supposed to be resting.' Liffey opened the door slowly so she could observe her aunt from the room's entrance hallway without being noticed. What she saw surprised her and it was hard to be surprised anymore by anything Aunt Jean said or did.

It looked like Aunt Jean was playing Project Runway, strutting up and down on her bed, hands on hips, like a model on the catwalk. After five back-and-forth 'walks on the bed mattress,' Aunt Jean fell over backwards and kicked her feet like a toddler having a tantrum.

"This is just great," Liffey groaned, "Aunt Jean has finally jumped off the cliff."

"Aunt Jean!" Liffey called. "What's going on? The doctor said you need to rest!" Aunt Jean did not answer. Liffey walked over to the bed and discovered that her aunt was fast asleep with little globs of dry avocado face mask dotting her chin like the stubble of a beard. She was snoring loudly next to Max who was also sound asleep.

Aunt Jean's current loss of consciousness provided Liffey with the opportunity to change quickly into street clothes from her solo dress and escape before Aunt Jean woke up and began to cry and moan again about how unfair it was that she had placed fourth in her Adult Reel competition this morning.

If Liffey was going to be successful convincing the stage monitor that she was a school newspaper reporter, she needed to look older and definitely more sophisticated. Liffey could wear most of Aunt Jean's clothes. She opened one of her aunt's enormous suitcases and found a black sweater dress. "Perfect! This is exactly what I need. Thanks, Aunt Jean," Liffey said under her breath.

She dug deeper down into the suitcase and came across black leggings and black fingernail polish. The only problem would be the shoes. Aunt Jean's feet were size 8 and Liffey wore size 6B. Fortunately, Aunt Jean had made Liffey pack her black ballerina flats to wear for dinners in Johannesburg. They would look great with the sweater dress and leggings.

Liffey had packed several appearance-altering props in her suitcase for emergencies: fake prescription glasses, a short blonde wig that Aunt Jean had given her on her birthday and dark pink lip gloss. She had bobby pins in her dance pack and tightly pinned up her long, light brown hair into strips around her head so the blonde wig would fit properly.

She evenly applied the black nail polish to each of her well manicured fingernails while her aunt continued to snore peacefully on the bed. Finally, when Liffey was satisfied that she looked at least seventeen years old and definitely 'east coast,' she applied the lip gloss, placed the fake prescription glasses on her nose, and walked out the door.

It was difficult getting her nerve up on the elevator riding down to the feis. The stage monitor Liffey had seen working the awards stage looked somewhat foreboding. She was a short, scrawny, tight-lipped woman who wore spectacles which would have better suited Mrs. Santa Claus.

Liffey wondered if the creepy voice she had heard from behind her earlier in the day when she was inspecting the trophies the first time had belonged to the stage monitor. 'I cannot believe I did not turn around fast enough to see who that voice belonged to.'

She took her BlackBerry out of her backpack along with the small notebook she always carried with her and the green Parker Pen her father had given her to write things down whenever she thought of something important she did not want to forget.

'I do look like a high school journalist,' Liffey thought, sucking in extra oxygen as the elevator smoothly arrived at its first floor destination. 'I need to walk with authority, like no one has ever said "no you cannot" to me,' thought Liffey, giving herself one final inspection in her compact mirror.

'I can totally do this.'

When Liffey arrived at the awards stage, she walked briskly over to the stage monitor who was standing stiffly at attention with her clipboard like she was the commanding officer of a firing squad. Dancers were asking her questions so Liffey politely stood off to the right and waited. When the stern woman finally noticed Liffey lurking next to her, she turned and quipped, "May I help you young lady?"

Liffey answered confidently, "Yes you can. Thank you very much. My name is Siobhan McKenna. I am the editor of my school's weekly newspaper, The Ben Franklin Reporter. We have several Irish dancers at our school who are Murphys and I would like to do a piece about the Murphy Family Perpetual Trophy for a feature story in next week's paper. Would it be possible for me to take a few pictures and gather a bit of information about the Murphy Perpetual Trophy competition? I will be very low key."

The monitor looked Liffey up and down, sizing her up. Liffey smiled hopefully.

"All right. Yes. I suppose you may take a few photos and gather information for your article. But make it fast. I do not want my dancers to become distracted by someone who has obviously read those Twilight vampire books one too many times."

Liffey tried not to flinch. She was not trying to look 'dark' in her black sweater dress, ribbed leggings and black finger nail polish. She was trying to look 'professional.'

She climbed up the stage stairs and immediately began snapping pictures of the Murphy trophy. After rotating the trophy to get every possible angle from all four sides and the base of the cup, Liffey was fairly certain she had photographed the entire chalice.

Liffey sensed that her photo op time was running out when she took one last photo of the inside of the chalice cup. She had not yet even begun to manually count the amber stones.

Then it hit her. '*How could I have missed something so totally obvious?*'

The engraved brass dedication strip on the trophy's wooden base said:

Liberty Feis: Murphy Family Perpetual Trophy.

*This is the Liberty **TORCH** Feis!*

"Miss McKenna."

Liffey was lost in thought staring at the Murphy Family Perpetual Liberty Feis Trophy.

'How could a family who was donating a perpetual trophy to a feis not even know the correct name of the feis? Had the plaque's engraver make a mistake and forgotten to add the word 'Torch,' or did the Murphy family give the engraver the wrong information?'

"Miss Siobhan McKenna!"

Still, Liffey knew from personal experience that it was often very easy to miss something obvious. Like in Saint Louis when she knew something was wrong with an Irish dancer doll but could not figure out exactly what it was for quite some time.

"Miss McKenna!"

A rude voice behind Liffey definitely wanted someone named Siobhan McKenna's immediate attention. Liffey wondered why this Siobhan McKenna was not answering. She turned around to see who was repeatedly calling for this Siobhan McKenna.

"Well it's about time you turned around, young lady."

She tried not to blush.

Liffey had completely forgotten that **she** was this Siobhan McKenna! "I'm so sorry. Please excuse me. I'm afraid I was busy composing my Ben Franklin newspaper feature in my head and just blocked out everything else."

The stern stage monitor, who was wearing a three piece pink Burberry plaid suit and matching shoes, softened up a bit. 'She takes this feis very seriously,' Liffey thought. 'She looks like a presidential candidate ready to give a speech.'

"I just want to inform you, Ms. McKenna, that the competition for the Murphy Family Perpetual Trophy starts on Stage 15 in 20 minutes. I am sure you will want to watch it. Remember, you are forbidden to take photos or video during the competition when the dancers are dancing but you certainly may interview them after the competition is over. The trophy will be presented, as I am sure you are aware, on this awards stage at approximately 3:00 p.m." Liffey nodded attentively.

"I am afraid you must wrap up your photo session on this awards stage within five minutes. I have a U-12 Prelim results group coming up."

Five more minutes was just barely enough time to count the amber studs on the chalice. Liffey raced back to the trophy and began the count, touching each stone as she went along. She also made a straight line in her notebook for each stone so she could double check her head count later.

There were 52 amber stones!

'I knew it! This might be the original Derrynaflan Chalice. As soon as Sinead's brother comes through, I will hopefully know for sure.' Liffey felt a keen sense of déjà vu because of what had happened to her at the National Portrait Gallery last summer in London when she had been counting pearls on a Queen Elizabeth the First portrait. 'There is no way I am sounding the alarm here and going

135

through that kind of circus again,' she thought. 'We could totally miss our plane to South Africa tomorrow.'

***

The media circus in London had begun when Liffey discovered that there was a problem with the Coronation Portrait of Queen Elizabeth the First in the National Portrait Gallery.

At the time, it had seemed like the entire London police force stormed the museum. Before she had been able to clue her father in as to what had happened, they were both hustled into a police van over her father's loud lawyer objections and taken to New Scotland Yard to be interrogated.

There had been cameras flashing and hordes of television reporters broadcasting live from Trafalgar Square. Newspaper reporters were frantic for information about what she had discovered and begged her to talk to them. There was absolutely no way she was ever going to stir things up like that again. The only good thing about that debacle was that Aunt Jean was not along with them on that trip. Liffey could not even imagine the kinds of things Aunt Jean might have said to live television cameras. She shuddered at the thought.

***

"With my poor Aunt Jean upstairs suffering from Post Traumatic Bling Disorder, I already have my hands totally full. I should just walk away from this chalice thing," Liffey told the little girl who had snuck past the monitor to watch her take pictures of the chalice.

136

"What do you think? If this *is* the real Derrynaflan Chalice, the secret stays with us until I figure out exactly what is going on," Liffey continued. "Agreed?" The little girl smiled and nodded.

Liffey remembered to take several close up photos of the beautiful metalwork on the chalice and even the inside of the chalice cup. When she heard polite coughing behind her, she knew it was the 'time to leave' signal.

"Thank you very much for allowing me to study the trophy," Liffey said to the efficient stage monitor who was still clearing her throat. "I am heading over to the Murphy Trophy competition stage now. See you later then."

Liffey was surprised at how natural she felt being Editor Siobhan McKenna. She had to try to remember to respond if someone else called her by that name.

On her way to the Murphy Trophy stage, Liffey received a text from Sinead. Her brother had flashed his detective badge and managed to get in to the National Museum in Dublin just as it was closing for the day.

No one seemed to think it was strange when he stood by the Derrynaflan Chalice exhibit and counted the amber stones on it like he was on a kindergarten class outing. Sinead copied Liffey with his text: *"There are 50 amber stones. Counted 3 times. BTW why does L need to know this?"*

Sinead also copied Liffey with her reply to her brother: *"IDN. L gets carried away with things easily ? a school project. 10X for help Big Bro. BFN."*

Liffey's heart was racing. The chalice in Dublin was a fake! It only had 50 stones and nobody had ever noticed. She wondered when and how the switch had taken place. And what she was going to do about it.

Liffey found Stage 15. It was surrounded by chairs on three sides. She was able to find a seat from where she would be able to closely scrutinize the dancers and the adjudicators. She would also be able to watch most of the audience.

Maybe if she was lucky, someone would look guilty or suspicious. She would need to take careful notes as to her own impressions of how well each dancer performed because the winner of this competition would receive the real Derrynaflan Chalice and take it home with them for a whole year.

Liffey had a strong hunch that being the best dancer here might not be what was really going on. The *best location* for the trophy to travel to after this feis might be the real objective of this competition. Probably to some place in New York since most of the dancers at this feis were from the area. But it could be headed to some place far away because there were dancers here from all over the world.

She would know which school the Murphy Trophy winner attended when the trophy was awarded. Liffey was positive now that whoever took the Derrynaflan Chalice from the museum in Dublin and turned it into the Murphy Family Perpetual Trophy was definitely several steps ahead of school newspaper editor Siobhan McKenna.

A middle aged man appeared on the stage. He made a few remarks about how important the Murphy family had been to the dance community in New York and thanked them for the perpetual trophy they had sponsored.

The musician started warming up on his concertina and dancers began to line up on the stage in a group of ten with at least 20 other dancers lining up with the monitor. This was going to be a long competition but Liffey intended to watch each dancer carefully.

The feis handbook Liffey began paging through as she waited for the dancing to begin devoted a whole page to the new perpetual trophy. It described the Murphy family as 'pioneers' in Irish dance and talked about their commitment to Irish culture and how the family was 'honored to present this living legacy perpetual award.'

Liffey wondered if she was the only one who noticed that this Murphy family information did not contain one single first name. Like a John, or Catherine or Joseph or *anybody* Murphy. It was also very vague about exactly what they had done as pioneers in the world of Irish dancing or how they had promoted Irish culture.

Liffey was deep in thought about how strange this Murphy legacy was without any first names when a glamorous, raven haired woman dressed in a pale blue silk dress tapped her shoulder and whispered in a catlike purr: "Are you saving this seat for someone dear? May I sit here?"

***

Aunt Jean woke up from a terrible nightmare about placing fourth in her Reel at a feis in New York. This of course was impossible. She shook her head from side to side as she crawled out of bed, trying to cast off the feeling of dread a bad dream often leaves behind.

"Liffey?" Aunt Jean called out. "Liffey, darling, where are you? We need to get dressed and then get to our stages."

The absolute quiet in the room was perplexing. Had Liffey gone downstairs already without her?

She hurriedly changed into her Irish dance attire, carefully centering her diamond tiara on her blonde wig. Liffey was probably off finding some breakfast. 'I never eat breakfast before I dance,' she thought proudly. 'The only nourishment I need before I dance is the air I breathe.'

The thought occurred to her that if she had time to spare before she danced, she would buy a rhinestone applicator from one of the vendors. She just might brighten up her dress a bit with some Swarovski crystals and rhinestones. Lots of them. 'One can never have too much sparkle,' she thought. 'Never.'

***

Liffey tried not to visibly shrink down in her chair in front of the competition stage when she heard a familiar woman's voice ask her if someone was sitting in the chair next to her.

She was certain that the voice belonged to the person who had asked her earlier in the day if she thought the gold and silver on the Murphy Family Trophy looked real. She regretted now having answered that question because she had inadvertently given this creepy lady a sample of her voice. Liffey wondered if the woman recognized her in the 'Siobhan McKenna' editor disguise. She suspected the woman did.

Liffey did not have to wonder long. "Haven't we met before, dear?" This woman was beginning to unnerve Liffey. "No, I don't think so," Liffey answered in a low tone, trying to disguise her voice as much as possible.

Liffey felt like a goldfish trapped in a bowl of water with a cat's paw swiping at it. "I'm sure we know each other, dear. I am Mrs. Sherlock. Think hard. Very hard. I am sure it will come to you if you think *hard*, Sweetie."

Liffey wanted to scream, "Sweetie?" and "Why should I think *hard*, *hard*, *hard*?" Liffey also wanted to say, "You probably know very well who I am and you are loving this jerking me around!"

Instead, Liffey said, "My name is Siobhan McKenna and I am absolutely certain I have never seen you before in my life until right now. Sorry!" This was actually true. Liffey had only heard the woman's silky voice from behind her. When she had finally forced herself to turn around, there was no one there.

'I need to get away from this head case right now,' Liffey thought, 'but I don't want to give up this great seat.'

Just then, Liffey saw her Aunt Jean passing by with an armload of merchandise and two tiaras perched high on her blonde wig which she had sprayed with red highlights.

"Oh no!" Liffey blurted out.

"Please excuse me! It's been really, really, really nice meeting you!" She nodded a polite good bye to the raven haired crone.

Aunt Jean was obviously completely out of control again. She was pulling a light-up, shocking pink, black polka dot suitcase. Her face was orange from another application of fake tan cream and her green sparkly eye shadow made her look like she was a contestant in an eye glitter pageant. She was wearing two wigs and each of her ears had six red 'gem tac' earrings. Her lipstick was an ugly peach cream tone.

'I knew I should have never left her alone,' Liffey thought guiltily, knowing full well she was going to ditch her aunt again as soon as she could get her back up to their hotel room and settled in.

'I did not follow the doctor's orders about how to treat Aunt Jean's Post Traumatic Bling Syndrome. I know I should be watching Aunt Jean, but I have to see this Murphy Trophy competition if I am ever going to figure out what is going on with the Derrynaflan Chalice. If Aunt Jean sits down next to me, it will attract major unwanted attention.'

Liffey went up to the stage monitor and was told the competition would start in exactly fifteen minutes. 'Just enough time to get Aunt Jean upstairs and myself back down here again. I will try to think of a good reason why I will have to leave the room again. I cannot miss this competition.'

"Aunt Jean!" Liffey called out. Her aunt stopped in the aisle and smiled. "Liffey, darling, where have you been? I've been looking all over for you!"

Liffey replied, "I've been looking everywhere for you too, Aunt Jean. Let's get back to the room and have a look at all the cool stuff you bought."

***

When Aunt Jean displayed her purchases, Liffey was delighted to see that her aunt had bought an electric rhinestone applicator. 'This will keep Aunt Jean busy for hours!'

She helped her aunt set up what looked like a mass production assembly line for applying rhinestones and crystals and raced out of the room. 'I'll deal with her bling disorder tomorrow on the way to Africa,' Liffey decided.

'I wonder how long it will take Aunt Jean to ruin this poor dress?'

***

Liffey was deep in thought waiting for the elevator. 'I know I am missing something here really obvious.' She had to mentally wrestle with herself not to repeat the word 'really' three times. 'That awful woman has totally messed with my head.'

'I wonder what the connection is between Mrs. Sherlock and the Murphy family? It's obvious that she suspects that I know something is wrong with the Murphy Family Perpetual Trophy.'

Who would have gone to so much trouble to brazenly display a stolen object in front of hundreds of spectators at an Irish dance competition? Why wouldn't the thief or thieves have just stolen it and then taken it to its final destination?

Why such an elaborate production number? A fake chalice had been substituted for the real one at the museum in Dublin. Then the real chalice had been disguised as a perpetual trophy at a feis. What was the point? Why was there such a public exhibition of a valuable, *stolen* artifact? Wasn't that risky? It was like advertising a theft.

'Risky.' Liffey knew that some people thrived on what her father, Attorney Robert Rivers, called "cheap thrills." He told her the story about how the famous Mona Lisa had been carried out of the Louvre Museum in 1911 by an irate Italian workman in broad daylight. This thief thought the painting should be returned to Italy where its artist, Leonardo da Vinci had painted it. So he removed it from the wall and walked out of the Louvre with it.

Did the chalice thief *want* to be caught? 'Possibly,' Liffey thought. After all, Liffey Rivers, a 13-year-old girl, had figured out it was the real Derrynaflan Chalice after calling Sinead in Ireland and having Sinead's brother count the amber stones on the fake chalice at the museum. It had been a total no-brainer. 'Even Nancy Drew could have figured this one out.'

***

Liffey walked briskly over to the Murphy Perpetual Trophy competition stage and was delighted to see that her seat was still empty and that Mrs. Sherlock had left. 'I knew she only sat down next to me to harass me.'

She was just in time. The first two dancers were center stage and ready to start. Liffey jotted down their feis competitor numbers so she could record her impressions.

"Well hello again, Sweetie. Nice to have you back." Liffey tried not to moan out loud. "Mr. Holmes and I were wondering if you were going to turn up again. I hear you are a reporter? Mr. Holmes told me he would gladly grant you an interview after the competition is over and he awards the trophy. He can give you background info on the Murphy family. He married into it."

Liffey decided that this might be just what she needed to sort things out. She pretended to appreciate Mrs. Sherlock's offer. "Thanks. That would be great."

"Good. Dr. Watson also agreed to be interviewed."

"Dr. Watson?"

Before Mrs. Sherlock could tell Liffey more about Dr. Watson, another woman tapped Mrs. Sherlock on the back and said, "Excuse me, ladies. Mrs. Baskerville is asking for you, Mrs. Sherlock."

"Thanks, Mrs. Hudson, I'll be right there."

"Are you ladies in some kind of role playing game club pretending to be Sherlock Holmes characters?" Liffey asked innocently.

She was completely unprepared for Mrs. Sherlock's uncontrolled, violent reaction. Mrs. Sherlock grabbed Liffey by her short, blonde wig and yanked it off her head.

"What in the world do you think you are talking about, Liffey Rivers?" she shrieked.

'How does that witch know my name?' Liffey felt like she might throw up.

There was a very loud, disapproving outcry among the spectators surrounding the Murphy Family Perpetual Trophy stage.

The musician, who had already begun to play the intro bars to the Hornpipe for the first two dancers, stopped cold. Everyone was looking at the shocked girl in the black ribbed sweater dress whose wig had just been ripped off her head by the old lady sitting next to her. Heads were tilted to get a better look, and the audience surrounding the stage was whispering among themselves.

"Mrs. Sherlock! For heaven's sake control yourself!"

"Whatever has come over you?" said Mrs. Hudson.

Liffey's head throbbed where the wig had been secured to her head. When color gradually began returning to Liffey's ashen face she could feel her cheeks flushing bright red with anger. 'Mrs. Sherlock is either totally insane or I touched a raw nerve when I asked her if there was a

Sherlock Holmes role playing game going on at this Liberty Torch Feis.'

Mrs. Sherlock, apparently stunned by what she had done, immediately handed the wig over to Mrs. Hudson who gently placed it in Liffey's hands and said with genuine emotion, "I cannot express to you how sorry I am that this terrible thing has happened to you, my dear. Mrs. Sherlock has been going through some tough times lately, and I am afraid she has been behaving irrationally."

'That's an understatement,' thought Liffey, 'and *how* does that creepy woman know my real name?'

"I'm just fine, Mrs. Hudson," Liffey lied. When she began to remove the bobby pins and take down the layered twists of hair which had been hidden under the wig, Liffey realized that she had a blinding headache. Mrs. Hudson gathered Liffey's hands into hers and said, "Thank you for understanding, dear."

It was when Mrs. Hudson extended her right hand for a final goodbye handshake that Liffey saw the yellow bracelet with brown speckles. "So, I see you are wearing a speckled band like the snake in the Sherlock Holmes short story, Mrs. Hudson? I recently read that story with my Aunt Jean."

Mrs. Hudson looked completely taken aback and Mrs. Sherlock shrieked again at the top of her lungs: "I *told* you she knows all about us, Melanie! *Now* what are we supposed to do with her? What's to become of us if we lose this round? It will be the end of us!"

Liffey was starting to get worried. What did Mrs. Sherlock mean when she said, "Now what will we *do with her*?" What did they think she knew? All she had done was

146

to ask them if they were part of a Sherlock Holmes role playing club because of their names. Each of them had a name of a character from a Sherlock Holmes story, and they had referred to others who were with them at the hotel as having names from Sherlock Holmes stories too. It was not rocket science to figure out that they might be part of some weird group.

'It's time to get away from these crazies. So much for watching the Perpetual Murphy Trophy competition,' Liffey thought sadly. 'I will have to stand somewhere in the crowd to watch.' When Liffey stood up and began to leave the stage area, she was acutely aware that all eyes were on her and that the competition had been delayed because of Mrs. Sherlock's assault.

Before Liffey could get away from the stage area, a uniformed police officer stopped her and asked her to come with him.

He walked over to Mrs. Hudson and Mrs. Sherlock. Liffey knew that if she called her attorney father, he would advise her to go with the officer, but that she should not say anything unless she had a lawyer with her, because sometimes innocent people can say something the wrong way or contradict themselves later.

Mrs. Hudson was holding Mrs. Sherlock's elbow trying to persuade her to leave, but Mrs. Sherlock seemed to be in some kind of trance and unable to move.

"Hello ladies. I need to ask you a few questions. I am Officer Malone. I have several witnesses who saw one of you ladies viciously remove a blonde wig from the head of this young girl. Would you like to tell me about it?"

No one in the audience was still pretending not to be listening and watching what was going on. The stage monitor looked like she was going to have a heart attack, and the word had spread to other stages. Soon there were at least two hundred spectators. Liffey missed Aunt Jean. Her aunt would certainly be no help whatsoever, but she was someone who cared deeply for Liffey and would at least offer some emotional support.

"Which one of these ladies tore the wig off your head, young lady?" Before Liffey could decide whether or not she should point to Mrs. Sherlock, Mrs. Hudson began to weep.

"Sally did not mean to do this, Officer. She has been having problems with depression lately and has not been herself."

"She completely had it coming officer," said Mrs. Sherlock, incriminating herself. "She is masquerading as a reporter at this feis and is running around trying to extract information from innocent people about the trophy award in this competition."

"So you admit then that it was you who forcibly removed the wig from this young lady's head?"

"Yes, and I would do it again in a minute! She needs to be taught *not* to sneak around pretending to be somebody she is not."

"Even if what you say is true, that gives you no right to physically assault someone. I am afraid you are going to have to come with me to the police station and give a statement. You are under arrest. You have the right to remain silent. You may call a lawyer. Anything you say from this point on can be used against you in a court of law."

Two more officers arrived as backup, and led Mrs. Sherlock away protesting loudly in her lovely blue silk dress.

"You *tell* him, Liffey Rivers! You *tell* him who you are and why you are pretending to be Siobhan McKenna!"

Liffey did not think she had the strength to hold out any longer about the fact that the Murphy trophy was really one of Ireland's treasures, the Derrynaflan Chalice. She had hoped to gather lots more evidence before she contacted the authorities, but Mrs. Sherlock had boxed her in.

When Mrs. Sherlock had been escorted out of the stage area, Officer Malone turned his attention back to Liffey and said, "What is this fake identity accusation about then? Are you in some kind of trouble, young lady?"

'Not until Daddy finds out I 'forgot' to tell him about this incident,' thought Liffey.

Liffey decided the best way to handle this whole thing was to just spit it out:

"I will admit, Officer, that I disguised myself as a reporter from a local high school named Siobhan McKenna so I could follow up on my hunch that the Murphy Family Perpetual Trophy here is really a famous, stolen antiquity from Ireland called the Derrynaflan Chalice. After the theft, it was replaced with a fake chalice in the National Museum in Dublin."

"You are not serious, right? Is this some kind of prank?"

"No Officer, it is not. I can prove it." Liffey cringed when she got the familiar 'isn't she cute,' condescending adult look from Officer Malone.

"Where are your parents?" he asked. Liffey was not going to ever go in this direction again unless she was forced. Instead, she politely said: "You can do your own

149

investigation, Officer. The real Derrynaflan Chalice, the one that is waiting in the results room for the winner of this competition, has 52 embedded amber stones."

"The fake chalice that is on display right now in Dublin, only has 50 amber stones. I can get a statement from Detective Michael McGowan in Dublin that he personally counted the stones on the fake chalice."

"Why then did he not report this himself?" asked Officer Malone.

"Because he had no idea why he was counting the stones. My best friend, Sinead McGowan, is his sister and she asked him to do it for me as a favor."

"I see. So you and your good friend Sinead lied to a police officer?"

Liffey could see this might be a big problem for herself and Sinead and answered truthfully: "Sinead did not lie. I did. I told her that I thought there was a copy of the Derrynaflan Chalice here in New York. Not the real one."

"I thought that, maybe whoever stole the original chalice in Dublin and had sent it here disguised as a trophy, had not counted right and attached the wrong number of amber stones on the fake one in Ireland. I have learned that thieves often do not pay enough attention to detail."

Officer Malone shook his head and asked Liffey to sit down and wait for him to return while he contacted Detective McGowan in Dublin to confirm her story. Liffey whipped her BlackBerry out of her backpack when the officer left, and quickly dialed Sinead. There was no answer, so Liffey left mail: *"Busted. Sorry I dragged U and bro into Derrynaflan chalice theft. More soon. <3 L"*

While Liffey was thinking she had better get back up to the room to check on Aunt Jean, an elderly man pushing an empty wheelchair passed behind the chair where she was waiting for Officer Malone. A damp square of gauze was pressed against her nose and mouth, and the sleeping Liffey Rivers was quickly transferred to the empty wheelchair.

***

Liffey's eyes were open but she could not get them to focus. Everything was blurry and the air she breathed in smelled like fingernail polish remover. Her mouth felt like cotton.

The last thing she could remember was being told by Officer Malone to sit down and wait for him while he checked out her theory that the Derrynaflan Chalice in the Dublin museum was a fake. Liffey suspected that she had been chloroformed by the person who was now pushing her jerkily down this long hotel corridor in a wheelchair.

An unsettling realization came crashing into her sore head: 'The real Derrynaflan Chalice has 54 embedded amber stones! Not 52 like I counted on the trophy here at the feis. Why did I tell Officer Malone that the chalice on the awards stage was the original Derrynaflan Chalice?'

'BOTH CHALICES ARE FAKES!'

'The one in Dublin with 50 amber stones and the one here on the awards platform with 52 stones.'

'How stupid! If I had only slowed down and been more careful and reviewed the online chalice information I got from the museum after I had counted the stones, I would have caught my mistake immediately!'

'Now I feel like I have two heads and four feet and I've been abducted by one of those crazy Sherlock Holmes people and I'll never find out where the real chalice is.' She could hear her father saying, "Haste makes waste, Liffey." She had been very sloppy in her investigation and could only blame herself now for her stupid, critical memory lapse.

Liffey realized that she needed to get out of this wheelchair and escape right now. If luck were with her, whoever was pushing her along this dimly lit hallway would be old like Mrs. Sherlock and Mrs. Hudson. She knew she could easily outrun either one of them even after being chloroformed.

It was important not to reveal that she was awake now or more chloroform might be administered to keep her under. 'These people are total freaks! They are seriously deranged. At least Officer Malone will come looking for me if I disappear.'

The wheelchair began to slow down and Liffey plotted her next move. 'I am fairly certain I can outrun whoever it is that is pushing me,' she decided, wiggling her toes.

The wheelchair came to a complete stop. Liffey jumped up and began to stumble down the long corridor as fast as she could. Her legs felt like jelly. She was going to have to do better than this if she was going to get away. She could hear heavy panting not far behind her.

'At least whoever is following me is totally out of shape.' She was beginning to feel the strength returning to her wobbly leg muscles and picked up her pace.

The panting grew fainter. It was time to risk turning around to see who had chloroformed her.

Liffey was dismayed, but not completely surprised, to discover that her pursuer was Mrs. Hudson and she was talking on her phone.

'She was so nice to me after Mrs. Sherlock had been arrested and taken away.' Now Mrs. Hudson was apparently carrying on with whatever it was the Sherlock Holmes crazies were up to.

Even though she knew better, when Liffey saw the Exit sign directly ahead of her she quickly entered the stairwell. She hoped Mrs. Hudson was not calling more of her mental friends and instructing them to intercept her.

The stairwell was well lit. She was on the 15th floor according to the number on the heavy metal Exit door. She tried not to think about what had happened in St. Louis. There was nothing to indicate that she was going to be pursued now going down these stairs so Liffey began to descend as quietly as possible. She wished she were wearing her ghillies.

After tip toeing down three flights of stairs, Liffey heard it. She was sure she heard a door quietly opening a few flights below her but there were no footsteps. This meant that someone was standing still down there waiting for her. She was about to turn back and retrace her steps when she heard another door opening above her. The one she had come through a few moments ago.

She was trapped.

Officer Malone returned to the Murphy Perpetual Trophy Stage immediately after he had contacted Detective Michael McGowan in Dublin and asked him to alert the National Museum about the possibility that the Derrynaflan Chalice had been stolen. Like Liffey had said, McGowan thought the Rivers girl was working on some kind of school project.

Liffey Rivers was not in the area where Officer Malone had told her to remain. He tried not to let his temper flare up. Teenagers today were totally irresponsible. Especially the younger ones. She was probably snooping around another stage.

Before Officer Malone could organize a search for Liffey, Michael McGowan called with an urgent message. His sister, Sinead, had just received a frantic SOS text from Liffey which said she had been chloroformed and was now trapped between two people in a stairwell in the hotel somewhere not far below the 15th floor.

Officer Malone immediately called his partner who was stationed in the front lobby and instructed him to climb the stairs noiselessly from the lobby and be prepared to apprehend a suspect just below the 15th floor who could be armed and dangerous.

He alerted hotel security and told them to barricade the front entrance and all the exits from the hotel and to station a guard at the entrance to the stairwell in the lobby.

"No one comes in or goes out of this hotel," he ordered. He ran to the elevator bank outside the main ballroom and pressed the 16th floor button. He then radioed his precinct station and told them to send backup for a possible attempted kidnapping. "Mrs. Sherlock," or whoever she really is," he said, "is dangerous and may not be released under any circumstances."

***

Liffey was surprised by how composed she was when it dawned on her in the cold, concrete stairwell that the

Sherlock Holmes role players probably had hidden the real Derrynaflan Chalice somewhere else. Possibly right here in this hotel.

'Why else would they be so interested in what I do? They must think I am some kind of threat after Mrs. Sherlock watched me counting the amber stones on the Murphy Family Perpetual Trophy.'

'But why would a group of role-players steal an artifact and then make two fake ones? And then display *both* of them publicly?'

It just did not make any sense. 'If they wanted to steal a chalice and then hope that the crime would not be detected when they replaced the original with a fake, fine. But what was another fake one doing here at the Liberty Torch Feis?'

Liffey could feel her heart fluttering in her chest. This time, there might not be a happy ending. Three people were hiding in this stairwell. Maybe the other two had weapons. Liffey already knew one of them had chloroform.

Just when she thought she could not stand the suspense any longer and had almost decided to make a run for it, she heard scuffling coming from below and a firm voice: "Get down on your knees and place both hands behind your head, sir." Almost simultaneously, a door crashed open right above Liffey and a voice she recognized as Officer Malone's said: "Well if it isn't Mrs. Hudson. Drop your purse lady and place your hands on top of your head. Nice bracelet."

Liffey heard handcuffs snapping on wrists from two different directions.

***

Aunt Jean excused herself and left for the coffee shop restroom when Officer Malone walked in.

"Well, Ms. Rivers," he said with a broad smile, "it seems you were right about the Derrynaflan Chalice. After Mrs. Sherlock, who is really Dorothy James, broke down under questioning, we got search warrants for an entire block of rooms on the 15th floor."

"Members of her decadent role-playing group call themselves, 'The Speckled Band.' Apparently this whole thing is an elaborate big money stakes role-playing game between two teams."

"The objective was for Team A to steal an artifact from the National Museum in Dublin and then place a Personal Ad in a newspaper with clues as to what they had stolen and where it could be found. The stolen object had to be on public display. A replica of the stolen artifact was permitted for the public display but the real item had to be hidden nearby."

"Take a look at this newspaper clipping we found hidden in Doctor Watson's room."

Liffey read the classified advertisement and tried to figure out the riddle.

PERSONALS
A flan from **Derry** is nice to eat
while watching dancers move their feet.
On foreign shores they reel and spin
for a lady who welcomes the tempest-tossed in.

156

"Team B had 10 days to figure out what artifact was stolen from the museum and where it was hidden. They never got here to New York. They are in Derry in Northern Ireland with expensive opening night tickets to a production of Shakespeare's The Tempest."

"They thought the Derrynaflan Chalice was going to be publicly displayed in The Tempest as a stage prop. 'The lady who welcomes the tempest-tossed in' actually refers to the Statue of Liberty. It's a line from an old poem. Team B figured out it was the Derrynaflan Chalice but missed the tempest-tossed clue."

"Team A was set to win over two million dollars. The game time limits would have expired after the Murphy competition was over at about the same time The Tempest curtain call would be happening in Northern Ireland."

"Mrs. Sherlock's team won but it will certainly do her no good. She thought you were a spy for Team B and that you were going to claim the prize for them."

"We apprehended an elderly man who calls himself Dr. Watson trying to leave the hotel through an emergency exit. He was carrying a suitcase with some interesting contents. Among them was the real Derrynaflan Chalice with 54 amber stones."

Officer Malone thanked Liffey and told her to keep in touch with him because she was both a victim and a witness in this Speckled Band case.

Aunt Jean returned and announced that she was hungry and bored.

"Let's get out of this dreary hotel and find a good restaurant. I'm completely famished."

157

"Me too, Aunt Jean. After we have dinner, let's see if that new Sherlock Holmes movie is playing somewhere in the neighborhood."

THE END

A Brockagh Book

ABOUT THE AUTHOR

Brenna Briggs is the author of the Liffey Rivers Irish Dancer Mysteries. She writes from Mineral Point, Wisconsin.

Other Liffey Rivers Irish Dancer Mysteries:

#1 Mystery of the Sparkling Solo Dress Crown

#2 Mystery of the Winking Judge

#3 Secret of the Mountain of the Moon

#4 In the Shadow of the Serpent

#5 The Alaskan Sun

www.liffeyrivers.com

17776914R00096

Made in the USA
San Bernardino, CA
17 December 2014